BLOOD-TRAIL

Led by the Pima to the place where Gato had been, they found a blood-trail, bright crimson drops already drying to black on pink and white stones. . . .

Late in the afternoon Swan reluctantly called off the chase. "There's not much use pushing on," he said. His voice rasped; for the past two hours they'd shared what little water remained.

"It'll take us the rest of the day to get down there and get the water we need to stay on his trail and most of tomorrow morning to get back here."

"We going to try again when we can come back outfitted?" one of the possemen asked.

"I'm going to be back on Gato's trail at sunup tomorrow, and I don't plan to give up until I find him dead or bring him back alive!"

GATO

by

MEL MARSHALL

A DELL BOOK

Published by
Dell Publishing Co., Inc.
1 Dag Hammarskjold Plaza
New York, New York 10017

Dell ® TM 681510, Dell Publishing Co., Inc.

ISBN: 0-440-12933-8

Printed in the United States of America
First printing—September 1980

Chapter
1

Until she heard the hoofbeats, Kahenee had given no thought to the long interval that had passed since she'd seen any of the other Cocopah women. Time flows in silence across the desert, and it was not the way of the village women to stay together when they went out to gather pitahaya fruits during the short season when these cactus apples are at their ripest. Each day the women walked together from the huts—a loose-knit, laughing, gossiping group—up the long slope from the river, but once they reached the mesalands that rose above the Colorado gorge, they scattered rapidly.

Kahenee was eating an especially ripe, juicy pitahaya apple when the swirling, hot afternoon breeze brought the momentary whisper of an alien sound to her ears. At first she thought it was a band of wild burros, strayed from their usual grassland grazing-grounds on the mesatops. When the wind shifted and carried the strange sound away, Kahenee dismissed it and went back to enjoying the fruit she was munching.

She had separated from the other women earlier than usual that day, intent on reaching a canyon that her mother had showed her, a place where the pitahayas grew profusely and where there was a spring whose water, though tasting like most desert water of underground minerals, was better and sweeter than the other springs in the vicinity. Moving quickly on strong young legs, Kahenee had soon outdistanced the others. In such a raw, treeless land, carved by canyons, dotted by mesas that rose abruptly, and broken by the shoulders of wind- and water-eroded buttes, the women quickly lost sight of one another.

Many of them, like Kahenee, were making for favorite places. Some of them moved fast, others slowly; some worked diligently to fill their *kiahas*, others neglected the carrying-baskets to eat greedily the first fruits they picked, savoring the sweet juice as it gushed under their teeth from the coarse pitahaya pulp. The few who filled their *kiahas* at once usually hurried right on back to the village. Generally, by the time a carrying-basket had been filled, the village was anywhere from eight to ten miles away.

Kahenee did not stop to pick or to taste any of the apples until she reached the canyon to which her mother had first brought her. Although it had been only during the last winter season that her mother had gone to meet with the Mighty One Whose Feet Do Not Touch Earth, Kahenee had no hesitation about returning to a place where they had worked and laughed together. Her mother had died quickly and without pain; she had been buried properly with all the tribal customs honored, and Kahenee knew she was at peace. She drank sparingly from the spring when she first reached the canyon, rested a few minutes from her long walk, then began to fill her basket.

There were even more pitahaya cacti growing in the canyon than she remembered from years past, and most of them were loaded heavily with egg-sized fruits protruding rosy-pink from the gray spines that surrounded their oval bodies. Kahenee picked rapidly, but not carelessly; she always looked closely before kneeling to harvest the apples to make sure there were no rattlesnakes or scorpions at the plant's base. Her basket filled quickly, and she leaned it against a rock before walking the few dozen steps to the spring. On the way she stopped and selected an especially ripe fruit, the one she was nibbling at between refreshing sips of water when she first heard the hoofbeats.

Although she'd dismissed them the first time as the noises made by wild burros, when the breeze changed again and she heard the clopping a second time, closer, Kahenee became worried. The Cocopahs had no horses; she knew that whoever was approaching was not of her people. Her first swift dart of fear came with the thought that the riders were Apaches, who now and then swept down from the eastern mountains to make swift, fierce raids on the river tribes.

Tossing the partly eaten pitahaya apple aside, Kahenee began to look for a place where she could hide. She was at the very tip of the wide canyon, where the spring burst from a fissure in the rocks and trickled into a shallow basin in the sunbaked earth forming a small pond. Around the pool the canyon walls reared up almost vertically, their only opening the narrow fissure from which the spring ran, and it was too small for Kahenee to get into. Except for a belt of coarse, green grass where the pond overflowed and trickled along for a few yards before it vanished into cracks in the soil, the only vegetation that grew in the canyon was gray-green cacti: pitahaya, a few bull's-tongues, and some tall, thin chollas.

Quite literally, there was no place of concealment in the canyon, no sheltering vegetation, no big boulders to crouch behind, no clefts in the steep wall. Kahenee did the best she could. She pressed herself against the wall in a crouching posture, hoping that the light tan of her willow-bark-cloth skirt would blend with the dun-hued rocks and cause the riders to overlook her if they rode into the ravine.

Very soon, in addition to the clattering hoofbeats she heard voices speaking in a tongue she did not recognize. The sounds came closer, and she could count the number of horses now from the broken rhythm of their walking hooves crunching on the stony ground. The men's voices took form in her ears, three different voices, three men on three horses. Then they rode into the canyon and she saw them. They were not Apaches as she'd feared, but white men, wearing gray shirts and red breeches and wide-brimmed, peaked hats. They reined in at the mouth of the canyon.

One of them, a big man with a blond beard, said, "Hell, there's no more water here than there was in any of them other cuts we stopped at. I say we better ride on down to that river and water the nags, then take out for the rendezvous."

"You need to sharpen your eyes, Clegg," another of the whites said. "I told you the horses were smelling water. Look at that patch of grass."

"Jared's got you, Clegg," the third man chuckled. "If that ain't a pool of water back there, I'll fry my saddle and eat it for supper."

Although these were the first white men Kahenee had seen in her seventeen years of life, she was too frightened to pay much heed to the color of their skins or even to wonder why they were there. In 1846 there were only a handful of whites, perhaps as few as ten, who'd traveled the Colorado's lower reaches. Like all the River People, Kahenee had heard of white men, but she did not know of the war that was already looming between the United States and Mexico, or that it had brought these U.S. Army scouts into the area.

Kahenee could not understand what the men said, but she could get a fair meaning of their talk from their gestures. When one of them, a lean man with a brown, curly beard, pointed at the spring, she realized they would be coming to the pond in a few moments and pressed harder than ever against the hot, rocky cliff-side, as though to force it to open up and embrace her.

As yet the soldiers had not seen Kahenee. They dismounted, took canteens from their saddles, but they had not stopped to examine the canyon closely after determining that it did contain the water for which they'd been searching. They pulled the reins of their horses over the animals' heads and started leading them in single file up the narrowing canyon floor. Just before the leader reached the spring, he saw Kahenee and stopped short.

"What's up?" the second man in line asked.

"We got company," the leader replied. "Look over against that side yonder. Indian woman."

"Well, damned if it ain't!" the second man exclaimed. He let his horse's reins fall and yanked the carbine out of its saddle-scabbard.

In instant reaction the third man in line unsheathed his carbine, too. The leader turned and saw them. He said, "What in hell you fellows think you're doing? It's only a lone squaw."

"I'm not worried about her," the second soldier said. "Where you see one redskin, there's apt to be more you don't see."

"Ah!" snorted the leader. "If there was any more of 'em around, they'd be at us by now. Put them guns back. All we got here's one female Indian. She ain't much more'n a girl, and she's not bad-lookin', either."

"Anything female'd look good to you, Jared." The second man returned his carbine to its scabbard and inspected Kahenee closely. "And you know something? She looks pretty good to me, too."

"Stand up, girl," Jared called. "Let's have a good look at you."

Kahenee gathered that she was being addressed, but continued to crouch against the canyon wall.

"She don't understand what you're tellin' her," Clegg said. He called to Kahenee, *"Ponerse de sus pies, mujer!"*

Since Kahenee understood Spanish no better than English, she still did not move.

"You reckon she can't talk?" the third man asked. He was the youngest of the three soldiers, little more than a boy.

"Oh, she can talk, I'd imagine, Billy," Jared answered. "But she likely don't understand anything but Indian-lingo."

While they talked, the three soldiers had been edging closer to Kahenee, leaving their horses standing with dangling reins. They were only a few paces from her when she found her voice and said, "I would leave you in peace. My people are not at war with your people, wherever you come from."

"Well, we know she can talk, now," Billy observed. "Even if it's only jabber-jaw."

"I bet she can do something better'n talk," Jared grinned. "And we sure won't have no better place or time to find out how good she does it."

"Aw, hold on, now!" Billy protested. He was newer to Army service than his companions. Jared and Clegg were professionals from the small United States standing army whose men had been scattered through the swelled-out ranks of volunteers that the army had started recruiting when the inevitability of a U.S.- Mexican war had become clear a year earlier.

"Just don't worry about the girl," Jared advised him.

Clegg chimed in, "Hell, Billy, everybody knows these Injun squaws spreads their legs for ever-who comes along."

Even though she did not know what they were saying, Kahenee could tell the men were discussing her, and their continued edging advance toward her was all the warning she needed. She leaped to her feet and began trying to scramble up the steep canyon wall.

Jared covered the distance between them in three leaping steps and grabbed her by the arms; Kahenee struggled, but her strength was much less than his. Jared got a firm grip on one wrist, then on the other. She fought until she realized it was useless, then stood quietly, arms pinioned in back of her by Jared's hands.

Like all Cocopah women, Kahenee wore only a split skirt of coarse cloth woven from the inner fibers of willow-bark. It was less a skirt than it was a pair of aprons, front and back, held by a leather waist-thong. Her black hair was long, cut in a square bang over her eyes and allowed to fall free behind her. Since she was unmarried, her chin had not been tatooed, though the lobes of her ears had been pierced to hold short strings of small white shellbeads. She shared the short stature and full, rounded body of all the river tribes, and when Jared pulled her arms back and down, her firm young breasts jutted proudly at the two soldiers facing her.

"Hot damn!" Clegg said, staring at Kahenee. "For a squaw she ain't bad at all!"

"I caught her," Jared said. "I get first whack at her."

"Wait a minute," Billy urged. "We better let her go and be on our way. We're supposed to be downstream before dark and meet up with the rest of the troop."

"It ain't gonna be dark for a long time," Jared retort-

ed. "And even if it was, when you run across a lone
squaw, you're a damn fool if you don't take time to
hump her. Now, you fellows get over here and hold her
in case she fights too hard for me to handle her by myself. After I'm through, you can decide between yourselves who gets next go at her."

Clegg was moving before Jared finished talking, but
Billy hung back. His help was not needed; it was not
the way of the River People to struggle against odds
that were clearly against them. Kahenee tensed, but did
not fight when Clegg ripped away her skirt and Jared
pushed her to the rocky, hard ground and fell on her,
nor did she cry out at the tearing pain that came to her
with his rough, heedless thrusting.

Jared looked up, his face twisted in a grimace of
pleasure and surprise, and told his companions, "Hey,
what d'y know! I got me a cherry!"

Kahenee barely heard the words. Her mind was
closed to what was happening to her; she concentrated
on ignoring the hurting inside her, on holding back the
cries that were rising involuntarily in her throat. She
lay supine and unresisting when Clegg took Jared's
place and, after his friends urged him on, when Billy
replaced Clegg. Then, because they were lusty men and
had been a long time without women, Jared and Clegg
returned to her again.

They finished with her finally. Kahenee did not
move, but lay naked on the ground, her eyes closed.

Billy frowned. "You don't think we've hurt her, do
you?"

"Hell, no!" Jared grinned. "She ain't hurt none.
Come on, let's get the horses watered and find the rest
of the troop. We go now, we'll catch up before the captain's worried enough to send a scout out lookin' for
us."

Only after the three soldiers had moved away from her and gone back to their horses did Kahenee open her eyes, and then only opened them in the tiniest slits. She watched while the men drank from the spring and watered their horses in the pond, then swung into their saddles. She did not stand up, though, until the thudding hoofbeats had died away completely and the still air of the dying afternoon brought no echo of movement to her ears. Then she went to the spring, waded into the cool water of the pool, and washed herself.

Kahenee had heard the older Cocopah women talk of rape; the Coyotero Apaches, the Mohaves, and Paiutes had through the years raided the Cocopah villages along the Colorado, and almost always the placid, unwarlike River People had been the losers. There were also tribal legends of two or three occasions in the far, dim past when Spanish soldiers out on scouting trips had stopped at the villages and demanded that the Cocopah people provide women for their camps. Kahenee had not understood fully what the other women had discussed, the fearful hatred and disgust they had felt, but she understood now. Despite this she did not pity herself. What had happened to her could not have been avoided, and once it had happened, could not be changed.

She thought of all these things while she brought water up in her cupped hands and let it trickle down over her body until she felt refreshed and cleansed. Then she tied her skirt on, picked up her carrying-basket, and started on the seven-mile walk back to the village.

Chapter
2

Kahenee's father, Hahkasel, had recently taken a new wife, and Kahenee had not yet reached a comfortable relationship with her new stepmother. The girl did not tell either her stepmother or her father of the rape in the canyon. Then the time came when she realized she was pregnant, and she took her secret to the only other relative she had, her aunt Masipa, her mother's older sister. Even then she did not tell Masipa the whole story. She confessed to her pregnancy, but did not add that it had been three white soldiers who either singly or jointly had fathered the baby she was carrying.

Masipa dosed Kahenee with the bitter potion Cocopah women used to prevent conception, a tea made by brewing together jojoba weeds and the roots of devil's-claw plants, but the drafts Kahenee swallowed were taken too late to be effective. The child grew within her, and in the early months of 1847 she gave birth to a boy.

Unmarried mothers were not rare among the River People. It was no disgrace for a single girl to bear a child—or even more than one. The baby did not damage her in the eyes of a prospective husband; in fact, it made her more attractive to be a woman of proven fertility. In all the river tribes of the Lower Colorado

Basin, however, the enemy Mohaves, as well as the River People, Yumas, Maricopas, Halchidhoma, as well as Cocopahs, it was the duty of the *kwalhidhe*, the shaman or medicine chief, to make sure the baby's father was a member of the tribe itself and of a clan different from the mother's.

Mothaho, the *kwalhidhe* of Kahenee's village, took a single look at her baby and shook his gray head. "This one cannot be Cocopah. It has come from an alien seed. Look at its hair, like golden sunshine. Its nose, long and pinched thin, its skin, soft and pink." His wrinkled eyelids slitted as he stared accusingly at Kahenee. "To give birth to such a child, you must have laid with a Forbidden One, a monster from the northern mountains. Is this the thing you did, girl?"

Kahenee did not answer him. She looked instead at the pale-skinned infant with its shock of hair almost as white as the fuzz of the cottonwood seeds that floated down from the trees late in summer. Kahenee knew that the *kwalhidhe* had just pronounced the baby's death sentence, and though she had looked at the child often since its birth a few hours earlier, she now saw the baby with different eyes. Suddenly her tiny son was precious to her, and while a truthful answer to the question of its parentage might save her own life, nothing she could say would change the death sentence the shaman had passed on the baby. She came quickly to a decision and returned Mothaho's stare without speaking. The *kwalhidhe* held his eyes on her for a long moment before he turned away and went out of the birth-hut.

By remaining silent Kahenee had chosen to die with her child. The women who had helped at the birthing wasted little time in leaving. To them both mother and baby were dead, and it would be pointless to give any further attention or care to a corpse. Kahenee's stepmother was among the last of the women to leave, but even after she had gone, Masipa lingered.

She said, "I am sorry, Kahenee. You should have told me before it was too late. If I had known in time that a monster had fathered your child, I could have helped you escape before anyone knew you were carrying it. Now there is nothing I can do."

"How could I know?" Kahenee asked.

"Is this thing not true that you lay with a Forbidden One?"

"It is not true. The baby was fathered by three white-skinned strangers riding horses. They found me in a canyon one day while I was gathering pitahaya fruits."

"A-yah! Three of them? How do you know they weren't monsters if they had white skins?"

"They were men, just like Cocopah men in all ways but their color. My boy will not grow up to be a monster."

"How can you be sure?"

Kahenee closed her eyes and did not answer her aunt. Soon she heard Masipa go too. For a long while the hut was silent, then Kahenee heard the door-cloth rustle and opened her eyes to look, wondering if it might be the death owl coming in advance of the time she would have to die. The newcomer was Hahkasel. He had hurried from his work in the family's maize plot when he heard the news and was streaked with creamy dust. He came to the blankets where Kahenee lay and looked down at her and the white-skinned baby.

"Mothaho told me what he has decided. Do not stay silent, Kahenee, tell him about the baby's father. They will take the child, but you will still be alive to bear other sons."

"I cannot give up my first baby. Look at him, how small and helpless he is. How can you ask me to do this thing?"

"Because even if our laws let him live, the baby could not be one of our people. He would always be an outcast and a shame to you." The words came hard and Kahenee could not tell whether her father spoke from his own convictions or because Mothaho had reminded him of the obedience owed to the tribal laws of the Cocopahs.

She tried to frame words that would soften her answer to Hahkasel, but before she could find the words in her confused mind the doorflap was pushed open again and three of the village's elder fighting-men came in. One stopped by the door, the other two came across the hut to Kahenee's bed of willow-bark-cloth blankets. Firmly, but not unkindly or roughly, they pushed Hahkasel aside and lifted the girl from the bed. One of them tried to take the baby from her, but she clung to it fiercely.

"Let her keep it," the man at the door said. "It is better for us that she carry the small monster herself."

Kahenee's legs were watery and weak when the two fighting-men set her on her feet on the hut's dirt floor and led her outside between them, but after walking unsteadily for a few paces, she felt her strength coming back. She shook their hands off her arms and walked unaided as they made their way between the low dome-topped houses of mud-plastered reeds. The men kept so near her that their shoulders brushed Kahenee's, and the third man stayed closely behind them.

News of what was going on had spread quickly

through the village, and the more timid of its hundred inhabitants had taken shelter in their homes. Those few of the River People who were still outside kept their distance and averted their eyes as the little group passed by. It was bad luck to gaze on the living dead, especially when one of them, although an infant as yet only a few hours old, was said to be a monster.

Wordlessly the three warriors led Kahenee away from the village, which stood on a broad semicircle of sand broken by hardpan lapped by the mud-red waters of the Colorado. High water time was near, and when the girl looked back for a final glimpse of home, she saw the men and women already hurrying to return to their work in the maize plots that lay between village and river. They had little time left to make the ground ready for the rising water which would cover the cultivated ground and wet it deeply so that when the waters receded and the seeds were planted, they would germinate quickly and well in the earth as it warmed under the searing sun. The River People had not learned to irrigate their gardens. If the river did not rise enough, they would spend long hours carrying water in clay jars or tightly woven baskets to wet the earth.

Kahenee looked back at the village several times as the men escorting her led the way up the slope away from the river. Then, when they got to the broken ground that rose more sharply to meet the mesaland standing high above the gorge, it was no longer possible for her to catch more than broken glimpses of the huts and the people moving about among them. Once they had reached the cliffs, the village was lost to sight completely. Here their going slowed. There were no more trails, and they made their way by vestigial paths that led along narrow shelves, wind- and water-cut

ledges that slanted upward across the faces of the almost vertical bases of the mesas above.

Much of their time now was spent inching along
these ledges, and they were climbing as much as walking. A cooling breeze had blown steadily on their backs
as they were going up the level slope, dry upper air
sucked down by the river, moistened, and sent aloft
again. On the high ledges the wind became fitful and
broken by scorching downdrafts that swept the shelves
and whirled around the boulders that stuck from the
cliff faces. Their progress slowed as they mounted
higher. The sun passed the meridian as they neared
the top of the huge mesa whose base they mounted,
and when the climb was at last finished and they
reached the plateau that spread level for a dozen miles
ahead of them, their shadows told them that midday
had passed. Now, though, they could move faster and
again walked abreast, Kahenee carrying the baby, its
face shielded by her long hair that she had draped over
the child. A man was on either side of her, the third
man once more walking close behind.

Kahenee knew all three of the men who were her es-
corts and would be her executioners, but she did not
know them well. They were of another clan than hers;
she was Mathachva, they were Akwaka; in the life of
the village clans tended to stay together for amuse-
ments and in ceremonies. The leader of the trio, he
who walked behind, was one of the Akwaka elders. He
was the only one who carried bow and arrows, the long
cottonwood bow of the river tribes, as long as a grown
man was tall. The bow launched slender shafts made of
arrow-weed tapered to a fine point that would drive
through the body of a deer or coyote and transfix a
man—or a woman—at a distance of thirty or forty
paces. The other two men carried short Cocopah

lances tipped with slivers of obsidian, and gnarled clubs of polished mesquite burl dangled from their belts.

Along the rim of the mesa which they were following the ground was undulating rather than precipitous. There were a few sharply rising bluffs to be skirted, and now and again a yawning canyon too wide to step or jump across took them on a detour from their steady progress northward, but they had no more climbing to do. The men did not try to hurry Kahenee, but suited their longer steps to her slower gait.

When the baby whimpered, she stopped instinctively and lifted its head to let it fasten its small, greedy mouth on a nipple. The men on either side of her looked back at the leader, and he peered over Kahenee's shoulder, saw the baby suckling, and made a sign to the others that they were to wait until the child had been fed. True, both baby and mother would be dead soon, but Cocopah tribal laws did not include cruelty, only the swift execution of those who broke them.

There was no conversation either between the men themselves or between them and Kahenee. All of them knew what their mission was, and even had the occasion been of a different nature, the country over which they moved was rough, broken, stony, and boulder-pocked; just moving steadily forward demanded all their attention. The effort of walking was enough, no need to waste precious breath on words that could have no meaning for any of them.

In the early afternoon they had to leave the mesa rim to skirt the base of a smaller mesa that rose steeply above the level of the bigger one on which they were walking. When at last they rounded the small mesa's base and returned to the drop-off again, they could look down once more into the river gorge. Its western cliffs were now shrouded in deep shadow, the river a thin, shining strip far away and deep below, snaking between wide sandy shores and bordered by the narrow belt of green cottonwoods, willows, and mesquites that marked its high water level.

With the sun in their faces the heat that had grown steadily greater as the day advanced was immediately intensified. Kahenee was thirsty, but the men had not brought water gourds along, and because of this she sensed that the end of their journey was drawing near. The men would not take her much further; the distance they had already traveled was greater than any she had ever made from her village before. The sun was dipping more sharply now toward the horizon, and she was sure they would not go so far that the men could not return to the village before nightfall.

Kahenee's speculations brought other, even less pleasant thoughts into her mind. She found herself wondering how her executioners would do their work, with lances or knives or clubs, and whether they would offer her a choice or simply go about their work suddenly without warning. Then she began wondering whether the men would bury her and the baby or leave their bodies exposed, to be mangled by coyotes and pumas before the hawks and ravens swooped down to pick their bones clean. She wondered if the men would kill her or the baby first and tried to decide whether she would prefer to die first and not be forced to watch the death of her firstborn son, or whether she would want to wait and watch and make sure the baby's death was quick and merciful. Slowly, as they approached the place where the mesa's rim dropped away into space, the thought formed in her mind that perhaps the *kwalhidhe's* sentence need not be accepted. It was not easy for her to reach such a conclusion, for the training of a lifetime had brought her to accept that the tribe's laws and customs had been set down in the beginning by the Mighty One Whose Feet Do Not Touch Earth and could not be questioned or changed.

More and more strongly, as the edge of the rim came closer and closer, Kahenee's thoughts turned to escape. She realized that to bolt and run would be wasted effort; she had no hope of outdistancing fighting-men in the prime of their strength. Even if she outran the two younger men walking beside her, there was still the leader's bow and arrows; these would reach her no matter how swift her running might be. She looked along the rim, trying to find a place where the drop-off was not so abrupt, but everywhere she looked the edge of the mesa ended in a clean-cut line between earth and sky.

One of the men at her side turned to look back at the leader. Kahenee turned her head, too, and saw the elder raise a hand and make the sign that signified "not now, but soon." Perhaps it was this that decided her, that brought her to the final conviction that one kind of death was no better and no worse than another.

She waited while they took a few more steps toward the rim; now it was only fifteen or twenty yards in front of them. Grasping her baby tightly, Kahenee bolted. She ran at an angle toward the rim, slanting her course for the wall of the mesa they had been skirting, hoping to find a ledge, boulders, a gully, and hiding place or refuge, any obstacle that would hide her from the fighting-men behind her.

Kahenee's abrupt burst of motion after such a long period of submissively walking with them caught her executioners off guard. The two men beside her grabbed for her, but she was already beyond their reach. Just as she got to the mesa's edge, an arrow from the leader's bow sang by her head close enough to pass through her streaming hair, but the arrow went on to sail out over the rim and drop into the gorge. She heard the men running behind her, the urgent padding of moccasined feet on the stone-strewn ground, but she did not look back.

At the point where the mesa ended and dropped away sheer into the river's gorge, Kahenee veered along its rim. She found a ledge going down and followed it for a dozen long, leaping steps. Then abruptly the ledge ended. Kahenee fell into space.

For almost twenty feet Kahenee plummeted down in an unbroken vertical drop. Her plunge ended when she landed, body still upright, on a steep slope covered with small rocks and dirt. This scree deposit had been a century in forming. It was a thick layer made up of small rocks that the short, fierce winter rains and the almost constantly blowing wind had loosened and dislodged from the wall of the mesa and from the smaller mesa that towered an additional hundred feet above the main rise. Its own bulk held the scree in place. The combined bodies of Kahenee and her baby were the heaviest weight it had ever borne. Seconds after Kahenee landed and destroyed its precarious stability, the layer of scree began to slide downward. It moved slowly at first, then faster and faster until it became a wide river of rock. Great dustclouds rose from it, were caught in the always present updraft, and billowed up the cliffside, spreading across the face of the vertical wall, the cliff, and the mesa's rim.

Kahenee felt the slide begin. She scrabbled frantically across the face of the steep slope, somehow managing to keep on her feet as the loose rocks rolled under them. As she moved she triggered new slides, small trickles that quickly spread to the main earthslip and became part of it. She was almost across the area of loose rocks when she stumbled and fell, rolling as she dropped so the baby would not be crushed, would in fact be cushioned by her own body under him. The flood of stone carried her down with it for a short distance, but as it widened, it pushed her out of the main slide to solid ground at one side of the massive expanse of moving rocks. Kahenee felt the earth grow firm under her back. She half rolled, half crawled away from the rock avalanche until she could grasp a straggly mesquite bush that clung to a fissure in a boulder that stuck out of the cliff face.

Below and beyond her the slide continued, an expanse of rock and loose, thin soil five hundred feet wide, rumbling majestically down the thousand-foot face of the mesa's base to pile up at the next horizontal shelf of the gorge. Kahenee clung to the mesquite bush as the slide exhausted itself, until its low-pitched rumble faded into an occasional scratchy whisper accented by the clickclack of a loose stone bounding here and there down the huge scar in the face of the cliff. In the stillness Kahenee heard the voices of the three Cocopah men coming from the rim.

"Do you see the woman?" the leader called.

"No. There is still too much dust."

A prolonged silence followed. Kahenee managed to wedge herself a bit more securely into the thin branches of the thorny mesquite bush and then could turn her head upward to scan the rim. Her situation was the same as that of the men; she could see nothing through the billowing dust. She did not know how long she lay still. Gradually as evening approached, the wind freshened and blew steadily rather than in gusts. After what seemed to be a long time, the air grew clear. Kahenee could now see the mesa's rim, but the slide had pushed her far to one side of the spot from which she had jumped. She was now shielded from sight by the overhang of the rim and the big boulder from which the bush spouted.

One of the men called, "It was a great slide of rocks. She was caught in it and was crushed."

"We must be sure," the leader called back. "Do you see a place where we can climb down?"

"Not even a mountain sheep could climb down," the man replied.

"It is the same where I am," the third man shouted. His voice was fainter than those of his companions; it came from far along the cliff.

"Then we must go on until we find a place where we can climb down and search for her body among the stones that fell," the leader said.

"Now, that would be a hard thing to do," the third man replied. "Surely she is buried very deeply. Even if we climbed down there, we might never find her."

Again Kahenee strained to see the rim of the mesa, to locate the Cocopah men so she could hide from them if necessary. Then she suddenly realized that if she could not see them, they could not see her and that as long as she did not move, she would be safe. She bundled her son closer to her breast and resigned herself to waiting.

Many moments dragged slowly by before Kahenee again heard the Cocopah men talking. The leader said, "A-yah. I see that you are right and I am wrong. There is no place for us to climb down, and in the great pile of stones below us we could not find the woman. The baby must indeed have been a monster, and the earth opened and took him back."

"What will we do, then?" one of the men asked.

"We will tell Mothaho that we saw both the woman and the child die."

"A-yah. It will be a true thing that we tell him. They could not have lived after they were caught in the crushing rocks."

"It will be a true thing," the leader agreed. "And we will say nothing to anyone, not even to Mothaho, of how they died. Is this thing understood?"

"A-yah," the others chimed together. "We will say nothing."

Those were the last words Kahenee heard the men say. She lay cradled uncomfortably in the spiky bush long after she was sure they had gone.

Chapter
3

Kahenee lay motionless while the sun moved across the pale, cloudless sky and a shaft of its bright rays crept into the shade where she and the baby lay sheltered. She touched the shielding boulder. It was coalhot and the wind swept steadily up from the river gorge as evening drew closer and drained the moisture from her body. The baby whimpered, and she fed it, twisting around so that she could hold it to her breast. She continued to use her long, thick hair to shade the infant, and after it had fed, it blinked happily at her, then went back to sleep.

Kahenee was thirsty, terribly thirsty. Now that she was sure it was safe for her to move she began looking for a way up the cliff. Her eyes saw what the Cocopah men had seen before they departed; if there was no way for them to climb down from the rim, there was no way for her to climb up. The slope below the boulder looked passable, though; it lacked the overhang that made ascent of the rim impossible, even if it was dangerously steep.

To free herself from the bush, Kahenee saw that she would have to hold the baby in one arm and swing down to the ground below the boulder with her free hand grasping the base of the mesquite bush. It took her a long while to get the courage for the move, but thirst drove her to it at last. She tucked her son into the crook of one arm, took a firm hold on the sharp-edged bark of the mesquite branch, and swung out over the slope. Her feet did not quite touch the ground, and she held on until her grip grew so precarious that she was forced to let go. She dropped the few inches until she felt the hard-packed earth under her feet and curled her toes downward in her flexible moccasins to anchor them while she recovered her balance.

When the soil did not slip and she did not fall, Kahenee gained new courage. She set out at a long angle to descend the cliff, picking her way with infinite caution, her toes digging in as best they could with each step. It took her a weary time to make the downward climb. Long before she reached the first level shelf on which she could stand upright without fear of slipping, her legs were bleeding from knee to ankle, scratched deeply from the many times when her feet had been unable to take hold in the steep mesa face. When she began to slide, she saved herself from falling by dropping to her knees and spreading her legs so the weight of her body would hold her in place until she could claw herself upright again with her one free arm.

After reaching the shelf, Kahenee rested. Her thirst was intense, and she tried to lessen it by tearing a strip from the willow-bark cloth of her skirt and holding it in her mouth after the fashion of the men who on long trips across the desert carried pieces of the willow-bark itself to chew on. The cloth started a small flowing of saliva, but it only moistened her mouth and throat without relieving the deep thirst that was generated by the daylong dehydration of her entire body. In a kinder land Kahenee might have found relief by sucking on a pebble, but the rock of the desert country was porous and filled with alkali and salts which not only intensified thirst but brought sickness to anyone mouthing them.

Nothing grew on the face of the mesa. Nothing alive moved over it except Kahenee and her child. The sun dropped lower and shade began marching up the slope she was on. Kahenee knew she should move faster, but between the danger of being caught on the cliff when darkness came and that of plunging down it because of a misstep taken in haste, she chose the slower danger. Inching, often crawling, she made her way off the ledge where she had rested and down the sheer face of the mesa until she finally reached the wide strip of level ground that sloped to the river. Nothing grew here, either, except a few straggling bull's-tongue cacti and some devil's-claw weed.

At best the bull's-tongue cactus was a poor excuse for food, but its pulp did hold such moisture as the plant could extract from the soil and air. Kahenee found a level spot on the ground shaded by a bulging boulder and carefully cleared it of small rocks and pebbles. She untied the thong of her skirt and wrapped the coarse cloth around the baby. She laid the boy on the spot she had cleared and began working on the nearest bull's-tongue cactus.

She had no tools except her fingers, so she carefully pulled each spine from a blade of the plant. It was a painstaking and tedious job, but each time she tried to hurry, Kahenee caught her fingers on some of the spines and had to stop and extract them from her flesh before she could resume working. Eventually the flat, thick, fleshy blade was cleared, and Kahenee searched the ground until she found two sharp-edged rocks. She pounded the bottom edge of the oval blade between these until she could twist it free from the mother plant.

Her goal was very close now. Her hands shook as she laid the cactus blade on the hard ground and with the sharpest of her rocks slashed at it repeatedly until she had opened a gash in its leathery outer skin. Then she could slip her fingers inside the cactus blade and scoop out its pulp and carry the pulp to her mouth a few stringy bits at a time. The juice that flowed when Kahenee chewed the cactus pulp was acrid, even bitter, but it was wet. As soon as she had chewed one bit of pulp to dry threads, she spat it out and began chewing another piece. By the time she'd reduced the cactus blade to a flat, thin layer of leatherlike outer skin, the taste in her mouth was terrible, but its membranes were moist, and she had slaked, if not satisfied, her thirst. Picking up the baby, Kahenee started across the shelf once more toward the river.

Darkness soon made walking difficult, even dangerous in that land so cut with gullies and ravines. In the deep dusk Kahenee came at last to a spot sheltered by a pair of canted flat rocks that had broken off at some time from a long-eroded-away shelf and remained leaning against one another like a tent. Under the rocks she smoothed a place to lie down. The baby whimpered hungrily, and she let him suckle. He went to sleep almost at once. Despite the growling pangs of hunger that came from her own empty stomach, Kahenee soon slept, too, her strength drained by the exertions and emotions of the day.

Several times during the night she woke up. Twice the baby roused her with hungry cries which quieted as soon as he was full of milk. Once she waked when some scuttering insect, a scorpion or tarantula, crawled over her bare thighs. In spite of the tickling of the creature's legs Kahenee lay motionless; it was too dark for her to see what the insect was, but she felt reasonably sure it would not harm her unless she tried to brush it away. The creature wandered around over her skin for several minutes, then dropped off to the ground, and she did not feel it on her again. Another time she was brought from sleep by the distant crying of an owl. She woke only long enough to wonder sleepily if it was the Death Owl voicing its anger at her escape, before sleep claimed her again.

In the shadowed gray dimness of the false dawn before sunrise Kahenee came fully awake. It was the time when she usually got up to begin her day's tasks, but this time there was no domed hut over her head, no stepmother to push her away from the cooking-fire and take over the preparations of the morning meal of maize gruel and boiled, dried mesquite beans. The thought of food caused Kahenee's stomach to heave convulsively, she moved, and the baby woke up. He whimpered and she picked him up. The infant began blinking blindly at her with his wise, old man's eyes when he felt the familiar warmth of her breast and arms, and he took her nipple noisily, sucking at her night-distended breast. Until the baby's satisfied gurgling belches told her its small stomach was full, Kahenee ignored the demands of her own, then she cradled the child in her arm and set out to look for food and water.

Across the vast Sonoran desert that fills the area between the Sierra Nevada and the Rockies and through which the Colorado River winds in its deep, rugged gorges, the hours just before and just after sunrise are the day's most active time. The night-movers—coyote, deer, pumas, kit foxes, skunks, mice, and rats—are returning to familiar spots where they will bed down through the day. The daytime creatures—lizards, snakes, and all the birds except the owl—are rousing

from the darkness and beginning to stir. A few of the
desert's inhabitants—tortoises, tarantulas, scorpions,
and most other insects—are indifferent to the changing
cycles of light and darkness and pay no attention to
them or to the changes they bring to the temperature.

Kahenee joined the day creatures in the gray light of
predawn. She was less advantaged than any of them;
her senses were dulled from having spent her life in the
relative ease of the Cocopah village. Because she had
never ventured far from the village, the ways of the
desert country and its inhabitants were for the most
part strange to her. On her first morning out she
looked without seeing at many of the things she would
later recognize as sources of food.

It was by accident that she found breakfast. A cactus wren fluttered up under her slowly moving feet, and
Kahenee stopped involuntarily, surprised. When she
looked down she saw the wren's nest with its clutch of
tiny eggs. Small as the eggs were, they were food.
Kahenee dropped to her knees and robbed the nest,
breaking the five thumb-sized eggs one by one and
eating with relish the unhatched baby birds they con-
tained.

Though small in comparison to her great hunger, the
eggs gave her body new strength and increased her
confidence. The baby's weight seemed less as she
moved along, her eyes now searching the ground for
hints of motion. A few grasshoppers had begun to stir
as the morning grew rosy with sunrise and the air
warmed; until the light improved Kahenee had not
seen them, for their folded wings matched perfectly the
color of the rocks to which they clung. When the grasshoppers began moving, she saw them and since they
were still sluggish, she caught them easily. Within the
distance of a hundred yards she captured almost a

dozen grasshoppers, eating each one as she caught it after pulling off its hard, spurred legs and leathery wings. Their solid bodies crunched tastily as she chewed them, and slowly her stomach filled.

Now Kahenee began to feel thirsty again. Her eyes searched the land ahead, but there was no trace of fresh greenery, no telltale patch of dark earth that marked the location of a spring. It was a raven that at last led her to water when it swooped down to drink from a depression in a huge flat rock where a small amount of algae-scummed water remained from the last rain. Kahenee drank sparingly, dipping carefully with a cupped hand from the miniature basin. Then, because she could not be sure when she would find water next and because the sun was already growing hot and her legs were still weak from the previous day, she found a place where a tall, jumbled pile of boulders offered shade and sat down to rest.

During the slow succession of days that followed Kahenee faced many new experiences, the most important of these being her sudden need to think and plan ahead. Quite literally, she had never before had any need to do either. Her sudden dash to escape her executioners had come as the result of the first major decision she had ever made, and the beginning of her wandering with her infant son marked the first time she had ever been totally dependent for survival upon her own unaided resources.

Life in the set routines of the Cocopah village where Kahenee had been born and reared was lacking in individual challenges. Its tempo was geared to the seasons; there were the major tasks of preparing the soil before the spring floods, the planting, the harvesting. There was the year-round job in which both women and men shared of setting the weirs in the river and clearing

them of the fish they trapped; the seasonal jobs of
gathering the purple-red bulbs of the woman's-tongue
cactus and the rosy-pink pitahaya apples. There were
other women's tasks: basket-making, cooking, and the
laborious job of preparing the willow-trees' inner bark,
shredding it into coarse fibers, and weaving the fibers
into cloth.

Kahenee's life was not different from those led by
the other villagers. The Cocopahs were a placid people,
peaceful and self-contained; they did not range far
from their mud-plastered reed huts and their cultivated
plots along the river. By the standards of the nomadic
Indian tribes the Cocopahs were backward. Their fighting-men did no raiding, but went into action only when
the village was attacked. The younger men hunted, but
infrequently, their efforts usually being confined to
chasing the deer that wandered into the river bottom-
lands, attracted by the crops in the village's cultivated
plots.

Kahenee's idea of the land further than eight or ten
miles from the village was so formless and vague as to
be nonexistent. She knew that along the river to the
south there were the Mohaves, to the north the Paiutes,
to the east beyond the mesalands the Apaches, for
these tribes raided the settlements of the River People
every year or so. She knew the names of some of the
southern tribes that lived beyond the Mohave territory:
Chemehuevi, Halchidhoma, Yuma, Pima; she had
heard that in the northern mountains lived tribes more
peaceful than the Paiutes, but if she had heard the
names of these mountain people, she did not remember
them.

She was very well aware that there were other Cocopah villages along the river north of her own and that
she must avoid going too near the stream until she

passed these villages. Mothaho's sentence made her an exile from any village of Cocopahs. From the first uncertain, puzzled steps she took after escaping from her appointed executioners, Kahenee's choices of a route narrowed to one.

She did not realize this until she had walked for several days. Then she saw that the terrain was changing rapidly. There was no longer a wide beach stretching back from the river; the stream flowed wild and swift through steep rocky banks that only lizards and snakes, hawks and eagles, creatures which crawled or flew, could overcome. The river was out of her reach, and the desert land between it and the ever more distant mesas was even more arid and barren than it had been further south.

In those first days of her slow northward trek Kahenee survived more by accident than through any knowledge of how to use the terribly limited resources offered by the barren land. She had no tools or weapons. Whatever food she found, she had to catch with her own hands, but starvation is a quick teacher. Kahenee soon learned to move more quickly than the lizards and grasshoppers that became her staples. These she eked out with grubs, eggs from the nests of ground-nesting birds, and an occasional scanty harvest of stringy, tough mesquite pods from one of the trees that had survived after being seeded from the droppings of a deer. She had no fire, nor was there fuel available if she'd had the means of starting one; all her food was eaten raw.

As it had been from the beginning, water was her greatest concern. As long as she stayed in the belt where bull's-tongue cacti thrived, she depended on them as her chief source of moisture. Though Kahenee grew expert at extracting the spines from the thick, glossy cactus blades, she could not escape all the spines they bore. The needle-sharp stickers pricked her hands and left tiny, almost invisible clusters of tip-spines in her hands when she pulled the main barb from her flesh. These festered and formed small pockets of pus, like baby boils, that throbbed and ached until she squeezed and broke them. The squeezing discharged both pus and spines but left raw sores on her arms and hands, and these were slow to heal.

As Kahenee moved north she left the bull's-tongue belt and entered a zone where only the treelike cholla cactus was found. These held no moisture that could be extracted. Kahenee went without water for one full day and part of another. Her mouth and throat grew dry; she found it increasingly hard to swallow the food she caught. Her skin began to grow uncomfortably taut as its moisture was drawn out by the increasing intensity of the sun.

Through all her own discomforts Kahenee worried more about the baby than about herself. So far the infant had not suffered too greatly. She now kept him wrapped in her skirt all the time so that his tender skin would not be burned, and she drew the thick folds of the willow-bark cloth up and over his head to shield his eyes from the brassy glare that bathed the land from midmorning until late afternoon. But still she worried about the child; Kahenee knew that unless she kept enough moisture in her body, she would be unable to produce the milk on which the baby's survival depended.

It was late afternoon when Kahenee stumbled into the shallow valley where the barrel cacti grew, placed by some whim of nature in an area where they were not usually found. She began to run when she saw the plants, their sides bulging out from the rounded domes that formed their tops. Before she reached the nearest cactus, she stumbled in her weakness and almost fell, almost let the baby drop on the hard, stone-studded ground. She willed herself to move more slowly, found a safe place to lay the child, and searched for a thin-edged stone with which to attack the cactus.

Opening the dome's top was a long job. Like all spherical cacti, the barrel cactus is completely covered with spines, and its leathery skin is almost as thick as the oaken staves of the barrels from which it gets its name. Opening the barrel cactus is not easy even with a sharp steel knife or an axe or hatchet. The top must be taken off without splitting the sides, for once the skin is cut or broken vertically, it opens along the ridged seams and the precious liquid the plant contains dribbles away and is lost.

Kahenee had only a thin stone with an edge that was rounded rather than being really sharp, and her arms were weak and shaky after more than a month of inadequate diet and thirty-six hours of dehydration. She hacked away at the cactus's top, paying no attention to the spines that penetrated her hands and forearms. Several times she had to stop and rest before she made a breach in the tough resilient skin, but once she had broken through into the plant's interior, the job was easier. She hacked away a triangular section from the top and pulled it from the cactus, ignoring the hundreds of spines that stabbed into her hand as she tore the skin section free. Now she could reach the interior and its watery pulp, more liquid than solid, on which her life depended.

Though the sun had beaten down upon the cactus all day, its interior was barely lukewarm; to Kahenee's hand it felt quite cool. She spread her fingers wide and worked them around until the pulp was well-bruised

and even softer than in its original state. Then she
cupped her hand and brought up a palmful of mixed
pulp and liquid which she carried to her mouth and
swallowed. It was bittersweet in flavor and very wet.
Kahenee forced herself to wait a moment before taking
another sip. While she waited, as precious as the liquid
was, she dipped out a bit of it and let it dribble over
her head and face and run down her shoulders and
breast in a blessedly cooling trickle.

She drank again, and yet again, until her shrunken
stomach felt tightly, uncomfortably distended. She
fought down a gagging sensation that swept over her as
her system almost rejected the unaccustomed liquid
flood. To take her mind off the cramps that were rip-
pling through her abdomen, she dipped her hands into
the cactus again to wet them and passed them over her
naked body. The sensation was so pleasing to her
parched skin that she did this once more, and by then
her stomach had stopped heaving. She managed to
swallow a few more sips of the liquid before going
back to where the baby lay.

She lifted the child and pulled the willow-bark-cloth
covering away from his face. The boy gurgled at her,
as babies do, and she noticed that his hair which had
been like white gold at birth was already beginning to
grow darker. She carried the child to the cactus, dipped
a hand into its liquid interior, and let the baby suck a
few drops of moisture from her fingers. This was the
first time the infant had tasted anything except
Kahenee's milk, and the thinly acrid flavor of the cactus juice caused the boy to pull away at first. Then he
accepted the strange new flavor and began pulling at
Kahenee's fingertips with his tiny lips as lustily as he
pulled at her nipples. When she took her hand away,
he objected with small cries. Kahenee let the baby suck

moisture from her fingers several times before he lost
interest and turned his head away. Then she put him
back on the ground and went to look for food.

By now she had learned many of the desert's ways.
As she walked, Kahenee searched the ground not only
for anything edible, but for small round stones that
would fly true to a mark when thrown. She picked up
several such rocks as she moved slowly across the shallow valley and was ready when she saw the lizard, a
large gecko, sunning itself on a boulder fifteen feet
away. Kahenee stopped at once, then began inching
toward the gecko. She selected a stone from the stock
she had gathered and when she had gotten as close to
the lizard as she dared, threw the rock unerringly. It
hit the gecko squarely and stunned it long enough for
Kahenee to run and pick it up and end its life by rap-
ping its head sharply on the hard ground.

Wasting no time, Kahenee pinched open the lizard's
skin on the soft, thin underside of its throat and ripped
away the belly-hide. After dashing out its intestines,
she pried away the skin from the lizard's sides and
back and gnawed at it until no meat remained on the
gecko's soft, flexible bones. She dropped the skeleton
and went on to look for another lizard, but this time her
hunting met with no success. She prowled the valley in
a series of expanding circles, but all she saw were two
or three fuzzy tarantulas and the path of a snake in a
patch of sandy soil. Disappointed, but her hunger no
longer a biting pang, Kahenee returned to her baby
and lay down beside him to sleep.

Chapter
4

There were more than twenty barrel cacti growing within a radius of a hundred yards in the shallow valley, and Kahenee stayed there until she had drained each of its moisture. Each day, though, she had to range further and further looking for food; even though the desert creatures were unaccustomed to human presence, they soon learned to avoid the places where they were hunted. Then the day came when there were no more barrel cacti, for once they have been opened the plants die within a day or so as the sun evaporates the liquid from their interiors. Kahenee knew it was time for her to move.

During the first morning after resuming her travels she felt better than at any time since escaping her Cocopah executioners. She was no longer dehydrated, and though food had been scanty for the last few days of her stay, Kahenee had become so accustomed to subsisting on a few mouthfuls a day that her stomach no longer griped when it was empty. She found neither food nor water that first day, and on the next day her ration was limited to three or four grasshoppers, but she still had found no water.

Now she began to weaken. Her hands and arms bothered her, for they were covered with cactus-spine wounds in all stages of healing, fresh angry eruptions on top of old half-healed scars. From her fingertips to above her elbows these festering sores pitted her flesh. Though each of them represented only a minor hurt, the cumulative effects of the hundreds that she bore was to drain her body quickly of its strength and resistance. The baby had grown heavier, and its weight on her tender arms brought a constant nagging pain as she trudged on through the hot, dry day.

She was beginning to tire quickly and found that she could walk only a short distance before having to put the baby on the ground to ease the throbbing of her arms and hands and to let her legs regain their strength. The hot, dry air was relentlessly draining from her tissues the moisture they had stored up while she stayed in the valley of the barrel cacti, but Kahenee bowed her head in weariness and trudged on to the north. When she stopped, she rested badly, and at night she waked often, for her milk was so scanty now that the baby was sharing her hunger and whimpered through the hours of darkness.

When Kahenee saw the gray of dawn she got up, let the child suck the few drops of milk it could pull from her now flabby breasts, and resumed her slow progress. Even at sunrise the air seemed hot; it rasped the parched membranes of her nose and mouth when she breathed. A small lizard raised its head as she plodded by it. Kahenee saw it, but the little creature was no longer than one of her fingers, and she had reached the stage of hunger when the idea of food repelled her in spite of the constant gnawing pangs that gripped her stomach. Stubbornly she moved along, a few slow, unsteady steps, a pause to rest, then a few steps more.

Long before the sun reached the midpoint between its zenith and the eastern horizon, Kahenee was totally exhausted. The land around her—boulders and rocks,

a few straggling cholla cactus plants, the pink- and yel-
low-streaked earth itself—wavered and danced in
something more than the heat haze that was already
causing the air to shimmer. She saw a patch of shade
ahead, cast by a massive boulder that curved inward at
its base, and managed to reach it. She had just enough
strength to put the baby down softly before she pitched
forward and sprawled facedown on the ground, too
weak to move.

How long she lay there, Kahenee did not know.
Consciousness came and went. Once she heard the
baby crying, but was too tired and listless to rise and
feed him. Her feet had swelled, they throbbed and
ached, and her whole body burned with an inner fire.
The baby cried again, louder this time, and Kahenee
lifted herself, rolled over to the child, and crawled with
him to the base of the boulder. Though the distance
was little more than a yard, it took her a long time to
reach a place where she could prop herself against the
rough base of the boulder to sit erect. She lifted the
baby's head until his mouth found a nipple and fastened on to it.

Her head was lowered, watching the baby's face,
when Kahenee became aware of an alien presence. She
looked up. Four husky fighting-men had come up
silently to the boulder and were standing looking down
at her. Though her eyes were blurred and her vision
dimmed, Kahenee could see the painted markings on
their faces clearly enough to know what they were. All
Cocopah children were taught from babyhood to
recognize the war symbols worn by the Shivinith, the
Paiutes, the fierce fighters who preyed on the River
People.

Kahenee was too weak and tired to remain erect and
return the unwavering stares of the Paiutes. Slowly she

let her head droop until her chin rested on her breast, waiting for the blow she was sure would come from one of the war clubs each Paiute carried. All the Cocopahs knew that Shivinith killed the River People mercilessly whenever the two met.

After a few minutes when no blow crushed her skull, it sank into Kahenee's hazed mind that the men were not going to kill her at once. They were, instead, talking about her and the baby. Though their language was not the same as the Yuman-rooted tongue the Cocopahs spoke, the two tribes had a few words in common, and Kahenee could follow the gist of the Paiutes' discussion.

"She is very sick. She will die soon. Let us go on."

"She is not sick with an illness, Shinabits. She is sick from thirst and from a fever. Look how the cactus spines have made her arms sore."

"Leave her, then, and take the baby. It is a boy-child, we need more fighting-men."

"No, Ahkeet. If we take the baby, it will die without her milk. If we want one, we must take both."

"You speak truth, Avote. Look, she is a young woman. When she gets well, she can do much work."

"Then you carry her, Mahdak. I don't want to be bothered."

"We are not in a hurry, Shinabits. We have enough food and water to feed her, even if we are on the trail another day longer."

"A-yehah. Mahdak speaks truth, Shinabits. After the great sickness during the cold-time that killed so many in our village, we need more young women who will bear children and more young boys to become fighting-men."

"This is a true thing you say, Avote. Let us take them back with us."

"I say no. Kill them both or leave them here, they will die soon after we go on our way."

"Who speaks with Shinabits? You, Avote?"

"I say we take them with us."

"Ahkeet? What do you think we should do?"

"If we must take the mother to get the boy, let it be done that way, Mahdak."

"You speak by yourself, then, Shinabits. Do you still say kill them?"

"I still say we should kill them or leave them here to die. But if you are all foolish enough to say differently, we will take them to the village."

All that day and for the next two days the four Paiutes stayed at the boulder with Kahenee. They gave her small regular sips of water from their gourds and then began mixing powdered maize from their belt-pouches with the water in increasing quantities until Kahenee was eating a thick gruel. When she grew stronger, they fed her small bits of chopped dried venison. At night the men curled up to sleep on the ground in a semicircle around her and the child.

Clarity of sight and thought returned swiftly to Kahenee as the clean water and nourishing food restored strength to her body and its youthful vitality responded and overcame the infections caused by the cactus spines. Her fever faded, she could stand and walk without trembling. On the morning of the fourth day they set out for the Paiute village. Though they moved more slowly than the men would have had she not been with them, five days of steady walking brought them to their destination in the place the Paiutes called Tumurru, the land of big rocks. The village itself was a cluster of two dozen wickiups built on a high spit of earth that extended into the Colorado a

short distance downstream from one of the river's big
northern tributaries.

It took Kahenee only a short time to discover that
the Cocopah tribal legends she had been taught were
more legend than fact. The Shivinith were not total
savages, thirsting at all times for blood; in reality their
life was remarkably similar to that of the River People
far downstream. Paiute men, however, did not share
the work of farming and fishing with the tribe's women
as did the Cocopah men. The Paiute men were hunters
and fighters, away most of the time, ranging west to the
Black Mountains for sheep, to the high northern
plateaus for deer, to the east for antelope. Two or
three times a year they went out in force to raid the
villages of the Hualapai or Supai in the southeastern
mesalands or those of the river tribes downstream.
When at home the men devoted themselves to making
weapons and practicing their use.

Farming, fishing, and all domestic jobs fell to the
women; much more than was the case with the River
People, the Paiutes looked on females as nonpersons.
Reflecting the adult attitude, Paiute boys ignored
Paiute girls beginning with early childhood. In the
Paiute villages there was a more complete segregation
of the sexes for social reasons than in communities
where young boys and girls were kept apart to guard
their morals.

Paiute fields were not as large nor their crops as
diverse as those of the river tribes further south. Their
chief crop was maize, a stunted variety of short stalks
and small heads that yielded tiny grains. Kahenee
worked hard in the maize rows, as well as on the weirs
along the river. She also worked at basketweaving, and
at curing skins—a skill she had to learn. She soon realized, though, that despite her status as a servant or

slave she worked very little harder than did the tribe's own women.

Mahdak had gambled successfully for Kahenee; during the course of a long afternoon spent tossing the knuckle-bones he'd won her from the other three men who'd been in the party that found her. His wife, Nankoweap, taught Kahenee the Paiute way of doing things and helped her to learn the language. It was Nankoweap, too, who provided Kahenee with proper clothing. The Paiute women did not leave their breasts exposed as did the Cocopahs, but wore long, plain, sleeveless deerskin dresses. And though Mahdak lay with Kahenee now and then—as did a few of his warrior friends after getting his permission—this did not seem to anger Nankoweap or to change her placid acceptance of the Cocopah woman and her son.

Young Hahksle—Kahenee had given her boy a name defining his kinship with her father and her clan—had not been harmed by the arduous journey that began on the day of his birth. He developed from babyhood into a sturdy child, his hair growing darker year by year until it was as black as Kahenee's, though somewhat finer in texture. Until he put on the narrow Paiute breechclout when he reached the age of ten, Hahksle spent his days playing naked in the scorching sun, and his skin became as deeply bronzed as those of his companions who had no white mixture in their Indian blood.

Mahdak had only daughters by Nankoweap and came to treat Hahksle as his own son, though Hahksle was not removed from Kahenee's care early enough to acquire the disregard ranging almost to contempt which boys born into the tribe came to show toward their mothers. When Mahdak did accept Hahksle and began to treat him as a son, he spent much time with the Cocopah lad during the periods when the fighting-men were not afield. He gave Hahksle instruction in the making of weapons and in their use, even to teaching him the secret poison made of the crushed bodies of red ants and scorpions mixed with mashed wild parsnips that caused Paiute arrows to be so feared. Under Mahdak's skillful teaching Hahksle became adept with the flint knife, the war club, and the short Paiute lance, as well as the bow and arrow.

After Hahksle donned the breechclout and was considered old enough to go out with the men on their shorter hunting trips, Mahdak extended the area of the boy's instruction. Hahksle learned to read tracks, even those almost invisible on the rocky, hard soil of the desert highlands; he learned to stalk animals and to wait in hiding for them to come within bowshot. Before Hahksle was twelve he had brought down both deer and antelope with bow and arrow, and in his thirteenth year he rushed in with his knife to gut a snarling, snapping coyote another hunter had wounded superficially with an arrow. In the mock duels in which the boys of his own age engaged Hahksle was more than able to hold his own ground.

Acceptance of the Cocopah youth was widespread enough for the old men to allow Hahksle to go with the party that went on the yearly trip to initiate fledgling warriors into full manhood. At the end of each winter the initiates were escorted by some of the fighting-men west of the river and north across the desert to a place where hot springs bubbled from the ground in a series of dark caverns. Here the ritual of achieving manhood was performed by the fighting-men. A few of the Paiute youths still too young to become warriors went along to learn and to do the work at the camp so the fighting-men and those who were becoming fighting-men could spend all their time performing the ceremonies.

Inclusion of Hahksle in the party did not change the attitude of the one man among the Paiutes who refused to approve of the Cocopahs' presence with the tribe. This was Shinabits who made no secret of his dislike for the two Cocopahs and lost no opportunity to speak harshly to Kahenee and to scold Hahksle. Shinabits's attitude was adopted by his son, Tuquinka, who had been injured during birth and walked with a sidling limp. In spite of his crippled hip Tuquinka took part in all the play of the village boys, including the mock battles and individual duels that were designed to sharpen their skills with weapons in anticipation of the day when they would be old enough to join the fighting-men on raids.

There came a day in the summer of Hahksle's thirteenth year when he found himself face to face with Tuquinka in mock combat during one of these games. Their sham fighting soon went beyond the stage of play to become serious and ill-tempered. They were duelling with war clubs, scaled-down versions of the weapons used by the men. The clubs were made from burls of mesquite or pinon-tree roots; a gnarl or knot formed the head, while the handle was tapered on the root stock or branch by shaving it with a sliver of obsidian or by slow, patient rubbing with a piece of wet deerskin dipped in sand. The men's clubs were three to four feet long, those used by the boys perhaps two-thirds the size and weight of the bigger ones.

Small-scale or not, the boys' clubs were still ugly weapons, and after he and Tuquinka had sparred for several moments in single combat, Hahksle belatedly recognized that Shinabits's son had lost his temper. Tuquinka was turning their play into a genuine fight.

Hahksle fought back, growing angry himself, becoming determined not just to protect himself but to teach Tuquinka a lesson.

Being both taller and stronger than his opponent and having more skill as well, Hahksle's opportunity came along. Tuquinka started a backhand swipe, a somewhat clumsy blow that usually Hahksle would have been satisfied to parry. Now he met Tuquinka's swing with a hard upward counterblow, causing Tuquinka's club to fly high above his head, and while the other boy's arm was still raised Hahksle followed the parry with a smash at Tuquinka's arm that landed solidly and snapped the bones in his forearm. Tuquinka's club dropped from his useless hand, and the boy shamed himself by leaving it on the ground, then disgraced himself by screaming as he ran toward his father's wickiup.

Shortly before sunset that evening Shinabits came to Mahdak. He said, "The Cocopah boy broke my son's arm. This is a bad thing he has done."

"Hahksle told me how this thing happened. Your son grew angry. He turned their play into a true fight."

Shinabits snorted. "You would take the word of a river-frog? All people know the Cocopahs are cowardly liars."

"Hahksle lives in my wickiup as my own son. I believe him."

"There must be payment for the injury he did Tuquinka."

"When boys play too roughly and one hurts another, it is nothing more than chance. Hahksle did not plan to hurt your son."

"There must be payment, or I will bring this thing to the old men."

Mahdak thought for a moment. While it was true

that the presence of Kahenee and Hahksle had been generally accepted by the village, the centuries of enmity between the Paiutes and the River People made the acceptance still conditional. He did not want to risk exposing the Cocopahs to an argument before the tribal council; the elders might sentence them to exile or worse.

He asked, "What payment do you expect?"

"Three baskets of maize and a deerskin robe."

"That is too much." Three baskets of maize would feed Mahdak's family nearly a month, and a good deerskin robe represented many weeks of effort in following and running the deer and tanning the hide.

"Then let the Cocopahs serve my family while my wife takes care of Tuquinka until his arm is whole again."

Again Mahdak frowned thoughtfully. "I would think of sending them to work in your wickiup for the space between full moons. No more than that."

Now it was Shinabits's turn to think. At last he nodded. "It is fair payment. I will accept. We have no debts between us."

For the first week life in Shinabits's wickiup was bearable for Kahenee and Hahksle. After that it deteriorated rapidly as verbal insults gave way to slaps and cuffing by Shinabits and his wife. At the end of the second week Kahenee found a chance to talk privately with her son.

"Hold your temper," she cautioned him. "I can see what Shinabits is trying to do. By mistreating us he is hoping to cause you to attack him. He is a man in full strength, and if you forget and strike at him, he will hurt you badly. Perhaps he would even kill you."

"I understand," Hahksle replied. "But I feel anger

when he slaps you or when his wife kicks at you to make you work harder."

"This thing is nothing. Always remember, we are strangers among the Paiutes. If they wish, they can send us away from their village."

"Would that be bad?" Hahksle asked. "If they sent us away, we could go back to our own people of whom you have told me so many times."

Kahenee had indeed told her son of the Cocopahs and had taught him the language of the tribe, but she had not yet told him the complete story of her death sentence. She looked down at her hands and arms, deeply pitted with scars from the cactus-spine wounds. "No. We cannot go back, my son. If we are sent away from Tumurru, we have no home."

"Then we will make our own home. Surely there is a place for us?"

"I know of no such place. Where would it be?" she asked.

"I have heard the men talk. In the mountains to the east there are people who let strangers join their tribe and live in peace."

"How can you believe what a Shivinith says, my son? Don't you know they are all great liars?"

"What will we do, then? I am getting angry with Shinabits. It was not my fault that I hurt his foolish son. Tuquinka was to blame," Hahksle said.

"Do not let anger rule you. Let us wait and see what happens."

Chapter
5

What happened in the days that followed was an intensification of the hazing that Shinabits and his family gave the Cocopahs. After an especially bad day when he had seen Tuquinka strike Kahenee, Hahksle's young pride could stand no more. In the early evening he took his mother aside away from the wickiup.

"We cannot stay any longer with Shinabits. If they mistreat us tomorrow, I will strike them back."

"No, don't do this thing, Hahsle. The moon will soon be full again, and we will go back to Mahdak's wickiup."

"But we will still be serving the Shivinith. It is time for us to go."

"Where? We have no other place."

"To the people in the mountains to the east," he suggested.

Their earlier conversation had started Kahenee thinking. She said, "There may be a place where we can live with people more like our own. I have heard the men of my village say the Chemehuevis make strangers welcome. And it is by the big river where our people have always lived."

"Where are the Chemehuevis? Do you know this thing?"

"I do not know. But if they live along the river,

surely we can find them. We need only to travel its
banks downstream."

"If that is where you wish to go, we will find it,"
Hahksle promised. "Tomorrow we will secretly gather
the things we need for the journey. The next day we
will start."

Kahenee and Hahksle left the Paiute village in the
way they had planned. Early in the morning Kahenee
went to Shinabits, basket in hand, and reminded him
that for two days she had not emptied the fish trap. At
the weir she waded out into the river, leaving clear
tracks across the stretch of soft sand that bordered the
stream at that point. When she was standing knee-deep
in the water, Hahksle ran across the sandy stretch and
joined her. As he ran, he made sure that in some
places his footprints overlapped hers.

Anyone from the village who came looking for them
would, they were sure, read the message of the forged
footprints as they had been intended to do. The tracks
in the sand could be interpreted only one way: that
Kahenee had gotten into trouble in the river's eddies,
that Hahksle had raced to help her, and that both of
them had drowned. It would not be an unusual story to
the Paiutes; the Colorado took a victim or two from
the village every year.

Wading downstream, Kahenee and Hahksle came
ashore where the stonelike hardpan would take no
footprints to betray them. The day before Hahksle had
made a secret trip to the place and had hidden his
weapons, full food-pouches, and water gourds for both
of them. They opened the cache and retrieved the gear
and, still walking where the ground was hard and firm,
mounted the side of the river gorge and headed south
across the high plateau.

Keeping the gorge on their right, the pair moved

steadily through the high desert. It was Hahksle's first taste of freedom, and he enjoyed himself like a young mountain goat just released from a tether. While Kahenee walked with a slow steady pace, he raced ahead, scampering up high vantage points to look behind them for signs of pursuit during the first few days, then as it became apparent they were not followed, to survey the land ahead for easy paths across the broken terrain.

Hahksle also ranged on both sides of their route in search of food to supplement the maize powder and dried venison in their pouches. His forays were just successful enough to encourage him to continue them. Twice he brought back big rattlesnakes, once a fat chuckwalla lizard he had killed by throwing his war club. Another time he found a spring of sweet water that bubbled up in a hidden canyon, and from it they filled their almost emptied water gourds.

Though the sun beat down on them as mercilessly as it had on Kahenee when she'd made the trip north more than a dozen years earlier, they covered in eight days the distance it had taken her a month to make carrying the infant Hahksle in her arms. Once they had lost their fear of pursuit, there was no need to hurry. They moved at an even pace, keeping closer to the river now, looking for the villages of the Chemehuevis. Kahenee did not know exactly where these villages were located, but did know that they were not far from the territory of the Mohaves who were even more greatly feared by the Cocopahs than the Apaches or the Paiutes.

It was a Mohave hunting party, roaming further than usual from home, that picked up the trail of Kahenee and Hahksle two weeks after the Cocopahs had left the Paiutes. There were five men in the group, and after they had found one faint set of footprints left by Kahenee and Hahksle, it took them only a short time to find a patch of soft earth that told them a man and a woman wearing Paiute moccasins were going south. Immediately the hunters changed their plans, which had been to seek deer on the high mesas, and turned to follow the trail of human quarry.

Hahksle still kept to the habit he had formed during the early days of their journey; he still ran up high vantage points to survey the land through which they were passing. In midafternoon from the top of a steep butte he saw one of the Mohaves. The hunters had spread out in a wide, loose line to insure against losing the trail; the hard ground made quick tracking uncertain. By spreading out, they also placed the small group in a formation that allowed them to swing quickly in any direction if their intended prey changed course. Since the Mohaves were spaced far apart, Hahksle saw only one of them, but even a single pursuer was enough to alert him to danger.

Recalling the war lessons taught him by the Paiutes, Hahksle dropped to his belly on the top of the butte before the Mohave caught sight of him. Lying prone, he scanned the barren land for other moving figures. He spotted two more of the Mohaves at once and in a few moments saw the others as they emerged from a ravine they had been crossing. Hahksle watched the men for a short while to be sure they were looking for the tracks he and Kahenee had left, then he snaked down on the side of the butte away from the Mohaves and ran to catch up with his mother, who had been moving on ahead of him.

"There are men behind us," he told her.

"A-ee! This is a bad thing. Are they Shinivith?"

"No. I cannot be sure, but they look like the Mohaves that Mahdak has described to me."

"This is much worse! Are you sure they are following us?"

"I am sure. They have spread out so they will not lose our trail."

"How far behind us are they?"

Hahksle frowned. Neither the Cocopahs nor the Paiutes had any precise measurements of distance; they counted by such flexible spaces as a man's step or an arrow's flight. He pointed to the sun and drew a short arc westward from it. "If we stay here, they would reach us when the sun has moved that far."

"How many did you count?"

Hahksle held his hand up, fingers spread. "So many. But there may be more I did not see."

"Then we must run swiftly. If we go toward the river, they may think we are of their people, going back to a village."

"No." Hahksle was better informed about tracking than was his mother. "They will know from our tracks that we wear Paiute moccasins. But we must still run toward the river. The ground is harder there, and we will find better hiding places in the rocks and canyons along the shore."

"Let us go, then."

They set off at a trot, trying to cross only the rockiest parts of the ground where they would leave fewer footprints. They were two, perhaps three miles from the rim of the plateau where the ground broke abruptly and became a maze of deep seams, shallow ravines, and rough canyons as it began its downward slant to the river. Hahksle kept a close watch behind them and did not catch sight of the Mohaves until just before they reached the rim. He and Kahenee had gained ground when they changed directions; the Mohaves were much further from them than when he'd first spotted the party. But now the Cocopahs could tell by the arm signals the Mohaves were exchanging that their pursuers had seen them.

"They will not need to spend time looking for our trail now," Hahksle told his mother. "But perhaps we can get away from them in the canyons by the river."

"A-ye-ah," Kahenee panted. "They are still far behind, and there are many places ahead where we can hide."

When they began scrambling down the rough, broken slope that lay between them and the river, though, Kahenee and Hahksle found their progress slowed. They could no longer run as they had where the ground was level. Here they had to pick their way cautiously, moving sideways almost as much as forward, skirting massive rock formations and treacherous slopes covered with loose rock. While the Mohaves were slowed, too, they maintained their speed better than did their quarry.

It was a grim and silent chase. Pursued and pursuers ran blind much of the time, losing sight of one another in the upthrusting crazy quilt of ridges and ravines broken by long curving slopes and sheer vertical cliff-faces. Many of the cliffs could not be descended but had to be circled by backtracking and climbing or by risking disaster in a long plunging run down a precipitous slope bordering the cliff. The Mohaves were persistent, and by the time the long descent had been completed and Kahenee and Hahksle stood on the hardpan of the river bottom, they had only a half-mile lead.

They were now out of the labyrinth of crisscrossed jumbled rises and ravines. The ground over which they

ran was hardpan, scoured clean and flat during the
weeks when the Colorado ran at flood. Occasionally
the solid footing of the compacted earth was broken by
a sandspit or a yielding patch of silt left when the river
receded, and here and there a rising shelf or rock
jutted above its otherwise level surface, but none of
these caused delay. The river itself was on their right;
sometimes its curving course brought the red waters almost under their feet, in other places the stream might
be a quarter-mile from the base of the slope along
which they ran.

If the long descent to the streambed had tired
Kahenee and Hahksle, it had also tried the stamina of
the Mohaves. The hunters were running apart now, no
longer in a compact pack, but plunging along individu-
ally in a loose single file with great gaps between each
of the men. Ahead Hahksle saw that the riverbed
curved sharply in one of its tortuous serpentines to
sweep close to a towering headland of solid rock that
had withstood the erosion of ages.

"We will find a place to hide when we go around the
cliff," he called to Kahenee. "We will let them run by
us, and I will attack them one by one from the back!"

"No!" she shouted. "Suppose the first one sees us?
You cannot fight five men at once!"

Hahksle took command. He shouted sternly, "We
cannot run ahead of them any longer! Let it be as I
say!"

Kahenee realized the youth was right and dropped
into the Indian woman's habit of obedience to the
male. She nodded, saving her breath for running, and
as they rounded the cliff, began looking for some opening in its rock face into which they might dart before
the Mohaves could see them. They ran on past several
small slits before they found one deep enough to hide

in. The opening into which they plunged was no more than ten or twelve yards deep, but its mouth was narrow and its sides rose sheer to the top of the cliff four hundred feet above their heads. The river's curving course as it swept around the headland brought its waters to within a hundred yards of the cliff's rugged base, an expanse of hardpan as level as a plank floor.

Inside the opening Hahksle pushed Kahenee toward the back and stationed himself just inside the mouth of the rock slit. Both of them pressed close against the rough stone surface of the towering wall as they waited for the Mohaves to pass by.

Hahksle held his breath as the first four runners dashed past the slit in the cliff without seeing them; the Mohaves were intent only on rounding the reverse curve ahead and once more catching sight of their victims. The fifth man passed, and the instant he went by, Hahksle darted out behind him, his war club ready to strike. The Mohave was running hard, and it took the youth a moment to overtake him. He was within a pace of the runner, his club poised, when the man either heard him or sensed the approach of an enemy. He whirled, Hahksle struck, but the instant of delay coupled with the man's unexpected turn threw Hahksle's aim off. The blow that should have crushed the Mohave's skull glanced down the side of his head tearing away an ear, but only stunning instead of killing.

Badly hurt as he was, the Mohave was drawing his knife as he fell. Hahksle moved in for a second blow with the war club, but the Mohave was on his knees, his knife hand coming up in a thrust at Hahksle's groin. Hahksle grabbed for the knife hand at the same time that his club was falling. The club shattered the Mohave's skull, but his knife had caught Hahksle's arm and opened a jagged cut that ran almost from wrist to elbow.

Hahksle staggered back, the sight of blood spurting from the first real wound he had known upsetting him for a moment. He was looking down at the Mohave's body, his mind divided between wonder, pride, and pain, when a shout ahead of him brought back reality. Before rounding the headland the next-to-last Mohave in the line had looked back to be sure the fifth man was following. He had seen the quick, fierce encounter, and Hahksle saw him turn and start back, heard him shout to the men ahead of him. The youth ran back to the precarious safety of the rock-slit.

"You are hurt!" Kahenee cried when she saw the blood running from her son's arm.

"It is nothing. I feel no pain. I can still use my bow." As he spoke, Hahksle was picking up his bow and quiver of arrow-weed arrows, their points tipped with small flints and smeared with poison in the Paiute fashion. He took a step outside the cleft and launched an arrow at the first of the approaching Mohaves. The arrow fell short, for the man was still out of range, but the runner stopped and waited for his companions rather than advance alone in the face of Hahksle's arrows.

Blood was welling steadily from Hahksle's arm. He stepped back into the cover of the slit. Kahenee was waiting, holding the carrying-thong she had taken from one of the food-pouches.

"Your arm must be bound up," she told him and in spite of his protests that there was no time, grabbed his hand and wrapped the inch-wide thong in a spiral around his wounded arm. The crude bandage stopped the worst of the bleeding, but drops of blood still ran down Hahksle's fingers when he nocked another arrow in his bow and stepped outside again.

Fifty yards away out of certain arrow range the four remaining Mohaves stood closely grouped in a miniature war council. There was no way that Hahksle could see to get close enough to them for a hit, and he had no arrows to waste on missed shots. He pulled back far enough into the rock opening to be unobtrusive and still be able to watch the Mohaves. They were in no hurry. Their quarry was trapped and unable to escape, their only problem was to decide on the best method of attacking.

While Hahksle stood watching, the four men split into pairs. Two of them held their places, the other two began walking in a wide arc toward the river. He realized at once what their plan was. The two who had remained behind would wait until the others skirted the stream and got beyond the cleft safely out of arrow range. Then they would make their way back to the cliff face, and both pairs would sidle along the base of the headland toward the slit. They would time their approach so that Hahksle would be forced to face simultaneous attacks from opposite directions. When he saw that several minutes would pass before the Mohaves were in position, Hahksle stepped back into the opening.

"They will attack us from both sides at once," he told Kahenee. "They are moving into place now. My plan was no good."

"You are not to blame," she assured him. "It was the best chance we had. If we are to die now, it will be because the time has come for us to die. What is meant to be cannot be changed." Calmly she began gathering the biggest boulders she was strong enough to throw and piling them near the opening of their refuge. "We will fight them together. Perhaps we can kill them before they kill us."

Hahksle's arm was beginning to throb and pulse and send waves of pain up to his shoulder. He picked up his bow to see if he could hold it and found that he could. He nocked an arrow and stepped outside the cleft. The Mohaves who had gone to the river's edge were now beginning to circle back toward the headland. He studied the curve of the cliff, saw that he could not reach his enemies with arrows as they approached. He looked in the other direction where the other two Mohaves were waiting for their companions to get into position and knew that his bow would be useless against them, too.

It would be war club against war club at the end, Hahksle realized. If the cliff's curve kept him from using his arrows, it would also deny the attackers the use of theirs. He was certain, though, that when they began their final approach, one man of each pair would have an arrow nocked and ready if he or Kahenee stepped into the open. Better, he decided, to stay in the cleft and force them to come through the narrow opening. He and Kahenee still had a chance; the slit was too narrow to allow more than one man to pass through it at a time.

"We must be ready soon," he told Kahenee. "They are starting along the cliff now."

Neither Hahksle nor his mother considered surrender. They knew that giving up to the Mohaves would only speed the moment of their dying.

A rock tossed from outside landed at the opening and rolled to a stop. It did not lure Hahksle to leave cover. He gripped his club more firmly, glad that the arm wielding it was not the one that had received the knife slash. Kahenee lifted one of the boulders from the pile she had assembled. There followed a moment of stillness, of waiting, the nerve-tingling pause that occurs in the few seconds before any combat begins. Then the body of one of the Mohaves filled the narrow opening. The man came in with his war club poised to strike.

Hahksle brought up his own club and on it caught the blow of the Mohave's weapon. The clubs met, the Mohave's bounced high off Hanksle's lighter club. Hahksle swung his club in a sidewise sweep that caught his foe's arm while he was raising it for a second blow. It was not a killing strike or even a crippling one, but it twirled the man around and threw him off balance. Before he could turn back, Kahenee threw one of her big stones. It landed squarely on the side of the Mohave's head, and he went down.

Another of the Mohaves was already pushing into the narrow cleft when the first attacker fell, and the second man was thrown back by the falling body of the first. Hahksle took a half step forward and brought down the gnarled end of his mesquite-root club on the second man's head. The Mohave dropped on top of the one who had attacked first.

An arrow from beyond the opening whistled past Hahksle's head, and he dropped to one knee in anticipation of a second shaft following the first, but there was not room for both of the remaining Mohaves to fire at the same time. The archer dropped his bow and hurdled over the prone forms of his companions, drawing his knife in midair. Still on one knee, Hahksle brought his club upward, a surprise blow he'd learned from Mahdak. The club landed in the attacking Indian's crotch and he fell, his back arcing with pain, but before Hahksle could get to his feet and step forward to strike again, the man rolled away out of the opening.

Voices sounded outside the cleft, shouting from a distance. The Mohave hit by Kahenee's rock struggled from beneath the body of the dead man that had fallen on him and turned to run.

Hahksle started after him, but froze when gunfire split the silence in which the fight had been carried on. Neither he nor Kahenee had heard guns fired before, and the ominous threatening blasts froze them into immobility. There were a half-dozen shots, then silence broken by a voice speaking a language strange to the Cocopahs.

"All right," the speaker called. "You folks can come out now. We killed all the Indians."

Chapter
6

Neither Kahenee nor Hahksle stirred. They stood for
a moment looking at one another in questioning
silence. They consulted by looks, nods, and hand gestures, and agreed not to move. There had been no anger or threat in the tone of the stranger's voice, but the
gunfire had startled and alarmed them. They watched
the opening of the cleft, waiting to see what would
happen next.

After a few seconds the voice outside the cleft said,
"A couple of you men cover me. I'm going to take a
look in there."

A gun barrel poked through the slit from outside.
Hahksle raised his club to knock it aside, but Kahenee
stopped him with a gesture. The face of a man, a white
man, appeared behind the gun. The man had a short,
straggly red beard and wore a wide-brimmed hat. One
of his shoulders was visible, covered by a gray shirt.
The man looked at the Cocopahs and let the gun drop
to a slant, its muzzle pointed to the ground. Hahksle
stood tense, waiting to act at the first sign of a hostile
move.

Over his shoulder the man called, "Hell, it ain't
white folks in here. Them Indians was after some other
Indians, a woman and a boy." Turning back to
Kahenee and Hahksle, he asked, "They was trying to

kill you, wasn't they?" When neither of the Cocopahs
answered, he turned again and in a louder voice called,
"Darnell! Come in here and see if they understand
whatever Indian-lingo it is you talk!"

A second man pushed into the opening. He was
dressed like the first, but his white face was clean-
shaven. In passable Yuman he asked, "Were the Mohaves trying to kill you?"

Yuman was the mother tongue, the root from which
the language of all the river tribes derived, so the
Cocopahs could understand the stranger easily enough.

With great dignity Hahksle said, "Yes. But we had
killed one of them. If they had not run, we would have
killed the others."

"Of course." There was more courtesy than conviction in the white man's tone. He asked, "Who are your
people?"

"Cocopah," Kahenee replied quickly, speaking before Hahksle could mention anything about the
Paiutes.

"You are far from home then," the man commented.
He turned and called through the cliff-slit, "We got all
the hostiles. These are Cocopahs in here, they won't
give us any trouble."

He pushed into the cleft followed by the red-bearded
man, who said, "Well, the hostiles is all we're supposed
to worry about. Come along, Darnell, we'll get on back
to the boat."

"We can't just go off and leave these people, Sergeant. There might be more Mohaves around."

"What d'you expect us to do? Take 'em back to the
fort with us?"

"I don't see why not. The boy's got a pretty bad cut
on his arm. Look at it. It needs attention."

"Damn it, Darnell, the U.S. Army ain't running a

dispensary for all the Indians in Arizona Territory. We're out here to settle down the redskins, not wet-nurse every redskin that needs doctoring."

"A little doctoring might go a long way toward help-ing settle them, Sergeant. These Cocopahs are way out of their territory this far north, all their villages are way on downstream. And we've got plenty of room in the boat."

"Well. All right, I guess it won't hurt to give 'em a lift. Tell 'em they can tag along if they're of a mind to."

Turning back to Kahenee and Hahksle who had been listening to the white men's discussion without understanding it, the soldier said, "We will take you in our boat to"—he paused, there was no word for "fort" in the Yuman language, and he finally settled for its closest equivalent—"to our village if you are travelling downstream."

Dropping into the Paiute tongue Hahksle asked his mother, "Is this thing true? Do the *hykos* have a vil-lage along the river?"

Kahenee shook her head, but there was doubt in her voice. "I do not know of one, but it is a long time since I left here."

"Wait a minute!" the Yuman-speaking soldier inter-rupted; he spoke in English, then went on in Yuman, "If you're Cocopahs as you claim to be, why are you talking in Paiute?"

"Long ago when my son was a baby, the Paiutes captured us," Kahenee explained. "We have escaped from them. Now we want to go back to our own people."

Satisfied, the man nodded and motioned for them to follow him. Outside the cleft a half-dozen soldiers were standing around. Hahksle looked curiously at the rifles

they were holding; his instinct told him these strange
long clubs were the source of the loud bangs he and
Kahenee had heard. He saw the bodies of the Mohaves
lying where they had fallen and wanted to look more
closely at them to see what kind of wounds the unfamiliar weapons caused, but there was no time. The sergeant was already barking commands, and the soldiers
began to move off in a straggling line toward the
riverbank. Darnell indicated that the Cocopahs were to
follow, and Kahenee and Hahksle joined the little
procession.

Boats were not strange or new to the Cocopahs. All
the river tribes and even the Paiutes made small craft
by lashing reeds together, more raft than boat, but
never had Kahenee and Hahksle seen a boat as large
as that of the whites, nor had they ever seen a boat
made from wood. The craft was built high in bow and
stern; midships it was wide enough to seat six men
abreast. The Cocopahs showed no surprise. They
maintained their composure as the boat bobbed downstream, carried by the swift current, kept in the chan-
nel by an occasional pull on the oars and by the
sergeant, who stood in the stern with a steering sweep.

Far more astonishing than the boat was Fort Mohave. It was a fort only by courtesy of title. It had no
walls, no stockade, and the only visible military charac-
ter it showed was the line of four mountain howitzers
that stood in front of one of the buildings. It was these
structures that impressed the Cocopahs, who had never
seen dwellings other than their own small domed huts
made of layers of reeds lashed together and barely high
enough for a person to stand erect inside them. To
Kahenee and Hahksle the fort's adobe buildings were
imposing edifices. They had windows, many of them
with glass panes, and each building had a door of

planks that could be closed against the weather or intruders instead of the willow-bark-cloth flap that served the Cocopah huts or the deerskin one used by the Paiutes.

Fort Mohave stood on a wide spit that bulged out into the Colorado. The spit was one of the few large ones along the river that was also high enough to escape flooding during the spring crest. The Yuman-speaking soldier, Darnell, who seemed to have appointed himself as guide and protector to Kahenee and Hahksle led them between the fort's buildings to the dispensary. The Army surgeon looked without interest at Hahksle's knife-slashed arm, but he unwound the leather strap with which Kahenee had bound the wound. He shook some crystals into a basin, added water, and swabbed Hahksle's arm with the purple liquid that formed in the pan. As the disinfectant dissolved the crusted blood and sank into the raw edges of the long, jagged cut that zigzagged like a lightning-bolt up his inner forearm, the burning of the liquid was more painful to Hahksle than the knife which had caused the wound. Hahksle did not wince, but held his arm steady while the surgeon bandaged the arm and dismissed the group with a flick of his hand.

Outside the surgery Darnell said, "I will give you bread and meat, you must be hungry. Then I will take you to some of your own people who live close by. They will help you find shelter until you are ready to travel on to your village."

There were no Cocopahs among the thirty or so Indian families who lived in the small settlement to which Darnell took Kahenee and Hahksle. Most of the reed huts scattered haphazardly along the riverbank just south of the fort had the flat roofs of Papago dwellings. The inhabitants included Papagos, Halchidomas, and

Chemihuevis as well as those who remained out of a group of eight families of the Bean People from the Salt River Valley far to the south. The Bean People had been hired by the Army at the Presidio in Tucson to accompany the soldiers who'd left there in 1858 to build and occupy the fort. Most of the original group had gone back home when less than two years after its completion the Army changed its mind about the need for a fort at that location and ordered it abandoned.

Even during its short life the fort had drawn settlers to its vicinity. Many of them were families heading for California over the new short route that swung south from Santa Fe through what was to become Arizona Territory who decided to stop at the Colorado. The Bean People, their work in helping to build the fort completed, had found jobs helping the new arrivals put up houses, as had the River People who joined them later. When the soldiers moved out of the garrison's buildings, the settlers lost no time moving in. Then, unexpectedly, the Army changed its mind; a new complement of troops arrived to reactivate the fort. When the military repossessed the buildings, the angry ousted settlers moved upstream to establish a new town, one they could call their own, but the Indians stayed. They went back to their jobs with the military; the men as guides, scouts, stablehands, and builders, the women as cooks, laundresses, and housekeepers for the barracks.

Kahenee and Hahksle were made welcome by the Papagos in the settlement and the Bean People were friends to all the world of Indians. There were two families of Maricopas and three of Yumas who had somehow found their way to the area and settled in. The Maricopas made the newcomers welcome, but the Yumas had an ancient tribal feud with the Cocopahs

and turned their backs on the new arrivals. That
Kahenee and Hahksle had survived as winners in a
fight with the Mohaves would have been enough to assure their welcome; the Mohaves were enemies of all
those along the river. They occupied the same position
in the southern Colorado basin that the Paiutes held in
the north, the Apaches and Navahos further east.

On their first night Kahenee and Hahksle were invited to sleep in the hut of a Papago family. Their
hosts urged them to stay, assuring them that there were
two or three abandoned dwellings which could quickly
be repaired. Hahksle followed his mother's lead in giving polite but noncommittal replies to the Papagos, but
Kahenee noticed his puzzled frowns and early the following morning led him away from the settlement
down to the river.

"Last night you did not understand why I said nothing about our plan to travel further," she began. "Is
this not a true thing, my son?"

"A-ye-ah. When we left the Shivinith, I had thought
it was in your mind to go back to our own people and
live among them."

Kahenee said sadly, "I have not told you many
things you should know." She extended her arms,
which still bore the pocks and craters caused by the infections of the cactus spines. "When you were smaller,
you asked me how I came by these scars, and I never
did tell you."

"That was before I learned it is a bad thing to ask
such questions."

"That is true," Kahenee nodded. "But listen to me
now, for I have much to tell you of the time that has
gone by."

While they walked beside the river, Kahenee told the
youth of his parentage, of her execution being ordered

by the *kwalhidhe,* and of her escape. She recounted the
hardships of the long trip north that began only a few
hours after his birth, and her discovery and capture by
the Paiutes.

"Now you will know why we cannot go back to
my village," she concluded. "Even though the old
kwalhidhe may have gone to be with the Mighty One
Whose Feet Do Not Touch Earth, whoever took his
place would still be forced to obey our tribal laws."

"But our people have other villages. Why could we
not find one of them where they would know nothing
about me?"

"No." Kahenee spoke sadly, but her voice was firm.
"This thing we cannot do. I am not sure where other
Cocopah villages can be found. Even if we did find
one, we could not be sure the *kwalhidhe* in it would
not know our story."

Hahksle said thoughtfully, "Then we have no place
to go."

"This is a true thing. It is why we must stay here.
Half of you belongs to the *hyko,* whose blood is in
your veins. If we stay, perhaps you can learn something of their ways as well as those of my people."

"Your people are mine too, my mother."

"Only part of you is Cocopah. The other part is
white. This may not be the thing you want, but it is the
way you are."

Slowly Hahksle nodded. "It is as you said when we
were waiting for the Mohave to attack us. What is to
be cannot be changed. It was not to be that we should
die, it was to be that we were brought here. Very well.
Let us stay here then."

Chapter
7

For the first months after their arrival at the fort, life was precarious for Kahenee and Hahksle. The planting season had ended before they joined the Indian colony there; weeks earlier the spring floods had receded and now the hot, hard ground would no longer germinate seeds. The Papago and Maricopa families of the colony were charitable; they let the two newly arrived Cocopahs help in their garden plots and gave them a share of the squash and beans their small fields yielded as well as sharing with them the dwindling supply of maize from the previous year's harvest. Though the sharing was generous, the supply of food to be shared was not large.

Somehow the Cocopahs survived, and gradually their situation improved. Darnell, the soldier who'd befriended them from the beginning, wanted to learn the Paiute tongue and hired Hahksle to teach him, but the ten dollars a month an Army private received left little enough to pay for extras; Hahksle got only ten cents a week for the lessons. Then one of the Yuman families decided to go back to their ancestral home; Kahenee and Hahksle moved into the hut they vacated and took over their garden plot as well. The Yuma man had been doing odd jobs for the sutler, and these fell to Hahksle. Kahenee inherited the work the Yuma woman had been doing, washing clothes and cooking for one of the companies at the fort. An enlisted man's mess was not included in the Army's table of organization; each soldier was issued a basic ration and expected to make his own cooking arrangements, and most companies pooled their rations in a barrack's mess.

Though the combined incomes of Kahenee and her son totalled less than three dollars a month, they were no richer or poorer in cash than were most of the families living in the Indian settlement. Two or three of the Papago families were rich; the men worked regularly as army scouts and trackers and received half the pay and rations given privates. The remaining Papagos had very little more than did the Cocopahs. When Kahenee began working at the fort, however, their rich and poor neighbors alike joined in helping them to assemble the clothing they would need. In the words of the commandant Indians who worked regularly at the garrison were required to "dress decently." This meant abandoning their native clothing and dressing like whites. The friendly Papagos and Yumans provided the Cocopahs with bits and pieces of cast-off clothing they'd acquired to enable Kahenee and Hahksle to take their new jobs. If any of the older residents of the Indian settlement resented the newcomers' having the employment they'd found, it was not shown by their actions.

Working at Fort Mohave thrust Kahenee and Hahksle back into the same sort of half-world to which they'd become accustomed during their first year with the Paiutes. Although the Indian village was less than a half-mile from the fort, it was only a marginal part of the garrison's life. The Indians who did odd jobs in the stables and barracks and officers' quarters were to their employers a part of the landscape, robot-conveniences who labored unnoticed.

It was not a one-sided relationship. The Indians made no effort to become familiar with the people they served; their jobs were routine and could be performed without instructions or supervision. Their real lives were lived in the Indian settlement. Vaguely they were aware that the whites of the garrison were members of a tribe that was fighting another tribe at some distant place far to the east, but intermittently recurring tribal warfare was no novelty to them. The Pagagos and most of the Yumas had a little understanding of English, but they paid no attention to the soldier-gossip about the Civil War; for that matter, the soldiers themselves knew little about the war and nothing that was current. News from the battle-fronts was two or three months old by the time it reached Fort Mohave; of all the Army's Western garrisons, it was the one most isolated by desert and distance.

By the time Kahenee and Hahksle had settled comfortably into the Indian compound Fort Mohave had little reason for existence. The Civil War had stopped virtually all movement of the emigrant wagons the fort was originally built to protect. The fears of an invasion of Arizona Territory by expansion-minded Mormons from the north or by Confederate sympathizers from California, which had prompted the fort's reactivation after its abandonment, had proved groundless. The garrison was never planned as a base of military operations, and with all other reasons for it being there at all wiped out, Fort Mohave deteriorated, neglected by the Army's Southwestern headquarters at Tucson, four hundred arid miles away.

Supplies arrived irregularly, but promotions and furloughs for its officers and men were forgotten. The soldiers performed routine military and housekeeping chores, sending out a scouting party now and then to show the Mohaves that their earlier attacks on emigrant wagon trains had not been forgotten. Idleness, the curse of all armies, prevailed. Now and then a soldier deserted and became the object of a cursory search; discipline grew slack. A few of the soldiers went looking for mischief, and some found it in the Indian settlement.

Kahenee and Hahksle had returned early in the evening from their work at the fort and were resting in their hut before going to tend their garden when the two soldiers pushed in.

"That's the squaw I been telling you about," one of the men said. "I had my eye on her ever since she begun cleaning our barracks."

Both Cocopahs had learned to understand a bit of English since starting to work around the white soldiers. Hahksle had a better knowledge of the new language than did Kahenee; his time spent teaching Darnell the Paiute tongue had resulted in him learning, if only involuntarily, a fair amount of English.

"This is our house," he told the intruders in their own language. "We do not welcome you here."

They ignored his words. The second soldier said, "She don't look no different than any other squaw to me."

"You ain't been watchin' her the way I have. She's a lot younger'n most of 'em and she don't run so much to fat."

"Fat or thin, a squaw's a squaw. About all you can say is they're better'n not havin' a woman at all."

Kahenee was remembering a day long past; she did not want to repeat the experience of her girlhood. She stood up and tried to push past the soldiers to the door. One of the men grabbed her wrists.

Hahksle's war club was leaning against the wall by the door. He took a step toward it, but the other soldier shoved him back. The man said to his companion, "Hell, we ain't goin' to do no good long as the boy's around."

"Git rid of him, then," said the soldier who was holding Kahenee. When the other man drew his pistol, he added hurriedly, "I didn't say to shoot him!"

"Wasn't aiming to." The soldier clubbed the revolver and brought the butt down hard on Hahksle's head. Hahksle dropped without a sound.

Consciousness returned slowly to Hahksle. The hut was dark. His face and head were wet, and though his head rested on something soft, it was throbbing as though a whole tribe of dancers was tramping inside it to the heavy rhythmic beating of dozens of drums. He lifted a hand to feel the pulsing in his temples, but his arm was heavy, and even the slight effort required to raise it set off white flashes like midsummer lightning inside his eyes and sent waves of pain to engulf his head and face. There was no strength in his muscles. He let his arm drop back without completing the motion he'd started.

Dimly, as from far away, he heard Kahenee say, "Lie quiet. The *hyko* soldiers have gone."

"How long has it been since they were here?"

"They left before the sun went behind the mountains, and it has been dark now for a long time."

Without understanding how the knowledge came to him Hahksle realized that he was lying on the hut's dirt floor, his head resting on his mother's lap, and that she was bathing his face with a scrap of wet cloth. He sat up, fighting the dizziness that accompanied his movements. Staying erect required too much of an effort, and he sank back on the floor.

"Did they hurt you?" he asked Kahenee. Because he already knew the answer, the words came from his mouth slowly as honey comes from a bowl after it has been chilled in cold water. Each time his lips moved, fresh pains stabbed at his head.

"They did me no harm from which I will not recover quickly," she told him.

Hahksle suddenly lacked the strength with which to ask any more questions. He closed his eyes. After a while the pain left his head and sleep came.

It was the last deep, effortless going-to-sleep he was to know for many days. Hahksle did not recover readily from the blow he had received. While none of his body muscles had been injured, his strength seemed reluctant to return, and there were many nights he did not sleep well or even sleep at all. On such nights Kahenee was aroused by his tossing and occasional groaning and came to kneel beside him. The first night she brought a wet cloth with which to bathe his still swollen forehead, but at the first gentle pressure of the cloth on his throbbing head Hahksle cried out with pain.

"If I hurt you, I am sorry, my son," Kahenee said contritely.

"It is not your fault. Every time I touch the place where the *hyko's* gun hit me, I hurt myself." He lay quietly for a moment before adding, "And bad things happen to me sometimes even when the place is not touched."

"What are these bad things?"

"Sometimes great clouds, like smoke, rise within my eyes, and until they leave, I cannot see anything. Sometimes it seems there are big plants growing in my head, trying to get out. Sometimes my ears are filled with the sound of bones scraping together."

"These are bad things indeed," Kahenee agreed. "But maybe when you get stronger the Mighty One Whose Feet Do Not Touch Earth will take these bad things out of your head."

As the days stretched into weeks, the huge swelling at the top of Hahksle's forehead subsided, though the area still remained tender and was painful when touched. There were still many nights when his sleep was broken, when the mere act of laying his head on the bundle of rolled rags that was his pillow set off the waves of pain. On such nights Kahenee was aroused by the low moaning that signalled the beginning of one of Hahksle's night attacks. She could only rise from her own bed across the hut and kneel beside him in silent sympathy, for he had learned that her gentlest touch brought him pain and that nothing she could do would ease him. She had tried all the concoctions learned from her mother, brews of roots and buds from desert plants the Cocopahs used as potions to relieve pain, but none of them had helped. Trying to find a clue to a remedy in Hahksle's symptoms, she'd asked him to describe how he felt when one of the attacks struck him.

"First I hear a murmuring like the morning wind that blows when the sun begins to heat the earth in summer," he told her. "The murmur grows louder and becomes a bubbling and roaring that fills my head so that I can hear nothing else. It is like the sounds I heard when I went with Mahdak to the *parishawamp-its*, the boiling hot springs that rise from the deep black caves in the mountains far to the north. The noise grows louder and louder until it makes my body shake and I begin to sweat. Then it suddenly stops, and I am sore everywhere and weak like a tiny baby."

After many days went by, Hahksle's strength gradually began to return. He heard the roarings in his head less frequently, and most of his nights became peaceful. They were not all peaceful, though, and during the dark, pain-filled hours as he lay sleepless and disturbed, Hahksle underwent a change.

In the past he had given little thought to the whites at Fort Mohave; he'd looked on them simply as the people of a tribe which had the strength to dominate an area. They had shown friendship and demonstrated their power by rescuing him and Kahenee from the Mohaves, and they had allowed them to survive in the settlement. He understood that the whites, like all tribes, had their own customs and tribal laws, and while living beside them it was both courteous and wise to observe these. As a stranger in the territory of a stronger tribe must do, Hahksle had adapted to the ways of the whites as he had to those of the Paiutes. If one of the *hyko* soldiers spoke to him sneeringly or brusquely or pushed him aside in the sutler's store or ignored him in the stable and blacksmith shop that were part of the store, Hahksle had interpreted these acts as being nothing more than the whites' tribal customs.

Until the two soldiers attacked him and Kahenee in their own hut, Hahksle had not considered them as being enemies. Now he began to think with anger of the men who had caused him pain. Revenge was not a Cocopah way; of all the tribes living along the Colorado River they were the most peaceful. Hahksle was not a typical Cocopah, though. Aside from the difference his half-white heritage made, his formative years had been spent absorbing the militant attitudes of the

Shivinith, and their credo was simple: Do unto your
enemies what you are certain they want to do to you
and strike your own blows first. And like the Mohaves
and Apaches, the Paiutes looked on everyone as an enemy.

Anger, growing bigger and stronger as night followed sleepless night, brought Hahksle at last to planning the blows he would strike. His Paiute teachers had
taught him more than the use of bow, war club, and
knife; they had impressed on him the need for planning
and patience. He began to study the fort's routines,
especially those that involved the two men on whom
his hatred had become centered. During idle intervals
between his odd jobs at the sutler's store and the
blacksmith shop he prowled the grounds of the fort,
penetrating into areas that were officially out of bounds
to Indians whose work did not require them to be
there. At night when all Indians were supposed to have
left the garrison's boundaries and returned to their own
settlement, Hahksle skulked silently, unobserved. He
went unnoticed into all parts of the enclave. Lax discipline made his prowling easy.

Many evenings he did not go home as he was supposed to when his work was finished, but hid in the
hayloft above the stable and at night dropped out to
slip ghostlike along the pathways between the buildings. He learned where the darkest shadows were,
where the sentries patrolled their beats, and the timing
of their rounds. On the rare nights when patrols had
been sent out and returned late, he peered through
slitlike barracks windows while the men cleaned their
rifles. He studied the motions the soldiers made as they
went through the regulation drill of unloading, cleaning, checking, and then reloading the big .45-.70
Springfield rifles they carried. Only after many weeks

of such observation did Hahksle actually begin to plan.

He needed two things: a moonless night and the assignment of either of the two soldiers on whom he sought revenge to one of the lonely, dark beats around the perimeter of the garrison area. With implacable patience he waited for these two needs to be met.

Even if Hahksle's mathematical skill had been great enough to allow him to compute the odds for or against the chances of his requirements being filled, he would not have wasted time calculating them. He simply waited until one of his targets was put on duty as a sentry along the back of the stable. This was Fort Mohave's biggest building. To accommodate the hayloft, its walls rose eleven feet from the ground, and for a hundred feet the back of the building stretched blankly windowless. Inside under the loft that extended for half the structure's width stalls divided the ground area into cubicles.

Only part of the building was used. Fort Mohave had originally been planned as a cavalry post, and the stable had already been completed before the planners discovered that the desert around it had no forage and its distance from other garrisons made it impossible for enough hay to be hauled for a mounted unit. The cavernous building now sheltered a dozen horses for use of officers, messengers, and scouts, and two teams of mules for supply wagons. The stable stood well apart from the fort's other buildings to minimize the offenses of its smell and its flies. In effect, the long, blank rear wall of the stable had become a boundary defining one side of the fort's limits.

When the night he'd been waiting for arrived, Hahksle slipped from the hayloft where he'd hidden during the late afternoon. Weeks earlier he had made himself a heavier war club than the mesquite-root

weapon of his youth, using a length of oak, part of a
spoke from a wagon wheel the blacksmith was repair-
ing. As he crept along the half-open front wall of the
stable, Hahksle hefted his new club experimentally and
wished he'd had an opportunity to test its balance at
least once in actual combat. He reached the building's
corner and merged himself with the shadows of its
eaves.

Sentries at Fort Mohave patrolled through the night
as prescribed by army standing orders for permanent,
unwalled garrisons located in areas that were nominally
peaceful. The fort's perimeter was divided into beats of
approximately two hundred yards each; the sentries
were required to time their pacing of this distance so
that alternately, first at one end of the beat, then at the
other, each sentry met the soldier patrolling an adjacent beat. Night duty was shared by two squads, one
of them on patrol from dusk until midnight, the other
from midnight until dawn. When relieved at midnight,
the squad on early watch returned to barracks, and
only the sergeant of the guard remained on duty
throughout the night. Regulations prescribed that the
sergeant check each beat at hourly intervals, but it had
been a long time since the fort had been aroused by a
night alarm. When the late watch had been posted at
midnight, the sergeant dozed in the dayroom until daybreak.

Hahksle did not leave his hiding place until long after he'd heard the early watch relieved. He stood
beside the stable, a deeper shadow in the building's
shadows, while the sentry passed him twice at a distance of only three or four yards, moved to the end of
his beat, and passed again on his return. The night was
completely still, its only noise the footsteps of the sentry grating on baked earth and the brief exchange of

words when one sentry met another at the ends of their
beats. Hahksle could hear the sentries talking, and
when the soldier on the beat passed the corner of the
stable, there was enough starlight to enable him to see
that the man passing was one of those for whom he'd
been waiting.

Slow minutes dragged while the sentry moved to the
end of his station and turned to retrace his steps. This
time the soldiers on each of the adjacent beats would
be at the greatest distance from the man walking the
beat between them. Anticipation after the long weeks of
planning and waiting seized Hahksle's emotions. He
felt his head swelling, his vision beginning to veil. He
forced himself to regain his calmness, to stay hidden
instead of rushing out to meet the approaching sentry
face-to-face. The sentry passed the corner of the stable
where Hahksle stood concealed. Hahksle stepped from
the shadows as soon as the man passed and took a
quick, noiseless step with moccasined feet. His club cut
through the still air of the quiet night. The sentry fell,
stunned, his rifle dropping to the ground with a dull
metallic thud.

Bending over the unconscious man, Hahksle drew
his knife—a *hyko* knife of good steel, bought with pen-
nies saved from many weeks of labor—and with a
single sweeping slash cut the sentry's throat. For a moment the Cocopah youth stood trembling, watching the
soldier's blood gush and puddle black on the ground.
The trembling passed, leaving Hahksle limp, relaxed,
and strangely fulfilled. He wiped his knife clean on the
dead sentry's tunic and sheathed it; then he bent and
fumbled for a moment with the man's belt before mas-
tering the buckle catch. He dragged off the belt with
its attached ammunition cartouche, picked up the rifle,
and fingered its hammer and trigger-guard for a few

seconds. The sound of distant footsteps brought him back to an awareness of time. He stepped back into the shadows at the corner of the stable.

Hahksle was totally without tension now or fear. His long time of planning during dragging days and sleepless nights had been wiped away in the catharsis of killing. He listened to the measured footsteps of the soldier on the adjacent beat as they approached and stopped, still distant from the stable. For several minutes the night's stillness was broken only by the creaking of leather and the shuffle of a bootsole on the ground as the sentry moved restlessly, waiting. Then the man called softly, "Dave? Dave? Where in hell are you?"

Hahksle moaned, a low muffled groan designed to carry only as far as the puzzled sentry. The man called again, a bit more loudly this time, "Dave? That you? Dave, what's the matter?"

Hahksle remained silent. Time lengthened, but he did not repeat his moan. The sentry called once more, "Dave?" and when he still got no reply, Hahksle heard the man's footsteps grating as he started toward the stable, his heavy brogans thudding scratchily on the hard soil. The footsteps came closer.

"Dave?" the sentry called again. His worried voice was still a low whisper. "Is that you—" Now alarm replaced worry in the man's voice. "Dave? What's wrong?"

Hahksle stood in frozen stillness and maintained his silence. He saw the sentry's shadowy form take shape, reach the sprawled body, and bend down over it. Only then did Hahksle move. A single long step brought him to the kneeling soldier. He thrust the muzzle of the rifle against the sentry's head and pulled the trigger. He was pleased when the man's body jerked convulsively before collapsing across the corpse of his companion. It was the first time Hahksle had fired a gun, and he had not been at all sure that the white man's weapon would work in Indian hands.

In the night's utter stillness the heavy rifle had roared with the effect of a cannon. Hahksle heard distant shouts rising from the other sentries. He wrenched away the belt and ammunition pouch from the body of the man he'd just shot, picked up the second rifle, and ran off into the blackness away from the stable, heading for the river.

Behind him the alarmed shouts were drowned by shots as sentries on other beats discharged their rifles at imaginary foes lurking in sinister shadows. Hahksle did not hurry. None of the shots was near enough to bother him. He trotted over the hardpan that the spring floods had scoured clean and the summer's sun had baked into a surface that would not take footprints. He stopped only once, long enough to sling one of the rifles on each shoulder as he'd seen the soldiers carry them when setting off on patrols. His heart was beating faster, but there was no roaring of dark waters in his head.

Hahksle felt no special sense of elation or triumph that his plan had worked successfully. He had known it would from the time he'd completed it. Ahead of him the Colorado glistened as its dark ripples caught and tossed into the night the rays of an occasional star. At his back the sporadic shots from Fort Mohave continued to assault the night's empty air.

Chapter
8

When Hahksle reached the water's edge, he stopped
to look back toward the fort. The scattered shots, after
increasing in intensity for a short while, were now dying down, to be replaced by the wailing of bugles sending alarm through the darkness. There were lantern
lights bobbing around in the garrison area, silhouetting
the figures of men scurrying between the buildings that
showed as black squares and rectangles in the reflected
light. In some of the buildings windows glowed yellow,
and the number of lighted windows increased rapidly
even while Hahksle was watching and listening to the
metallic warning shrieks of the bugles.

He stepped into the river and waded until he stood
knee-deep in the shallow, eddying inshore currents,
then began working his way downstream. He passed
the Indian settlement on the bank, low humps sensed
rather than seen, for no lights were showing from the
huts. Below the huts a long spit of hardpan stretched
fingerlike into the river, and Hahksle waded up onto it.
He picked his way along the narrow strand of stone-
hard earth and stood at its end where it widened as it
joined the bank, waiting for the fitful night breeze to
dry his moccasins. He was distant from the fort now; it
was visible only as a small glow against the dark sky,
and the sounds of excitement could no longer be heard.

When at last Hahksle's moccasins were so dry that they would leave no wet smudges on the ground, he walked to the settlement, carrying the rifles and belts. Kahenee was awake when he slipped into the hut.

"Those are soldier's guns you have," she said in a whisper.

"Yes." Hahksle did not bother to lower his voice, it rang out loudly in the little room.

"I heard a noise of shooting," she went on.

"I shot. Two of the bluecoats are dead."

"They were those who came to our house?"

"One was. I have not killed the other. Not yet."

"Why? Why did you kill them?"

"They harmed us," Hahksle replied simply. He turned away from his mother and began to pull apart the reeds that formed the hut's low walls, making a long crack in them in which to hide the rifles.

Kahenee watched him in silence. Hahksle had become a man, and it was not the place of a Cocopah woman to question the actions of a man—even though the man was her son. At last she said, "The soldiers will find out you have done this thing. Then they will kill you."

"They will not find out. I left no tracks. They will blame the Mohaves." Hahksle gave a final pat to the layer of reeds that now concealed his newly acquired weapons and lay down on his blankets. The strength that had flowed through his body while waiting for the sentries and the intoxicating exultation that had swept over him in the moments of their deaths had passed. He felt drained and weak. He said, "We will not talk of this thing again. I want to sleep now."

Hahksle's judgment proved sound. The Mohaves held the reputation of being the fighters among the river tribes, and, as is so often the case, blame went where reputation was. Although the Papago and Pima trackers found no signs that would offer clues to the identity of the sentries' killer, the fort's officers were unanimous in agreeing that the murders must have been committed by a band of roaming Mohaves. In fact, they told one another, the Mohave band was more than likely still hiding in the vicinity, watching for a chance to strike again. Both officers and men became more and more edgy. Soldiers walked night sentry beats in pairs. They began seeing hostile Mohaves hiding in every shadow and now and then let off a shot at one of them. The sergeant of the guard found no time to doze in the dayroom as alarm piled on top of alarm from early dark until dawn.

Firmly committed to the theory that they were threatened by enemies hiding in the high desert country around the fort, neither the officers nor soldiers seemed bothered by the close presence of the Indians in the settlement. The Papagos had always been peaceful and cooperative, as had the Yumas, and though a patrol did make a token inspection trip through the village, its primary purpose was to ask the occupants of the huts if they'd seen any signs of the band of five or six Mohaves that was now believed to be in the area. It was the only effort made by the Army to check out the settlement. The main effort made to find the mysterious killer was the daily dispatching of patrols to search a constantly expanding arc east of the garrison.

Hahksle saw the opportunity the patrols offered him. While the settlement slept and the garrison dozed fitfully, he slipped through the darkness carrying one of the rifles and an ammunition cartouche which he hid in a cave in the area the patrols were scouting. Then he waited until the second soldier on his deathlist went out with one of the patrols.

Deserting his job at the sutler's, Hahksle circled wide ahead of the patrol to retrieve the hidden rifle. He used the tricks of desert concealment taught him by the Paiutes to let the soldiers pass him. They moved in a line of skirmishers' formation, the men spaced fifty feet apart, avoiding the clumps of ocotillo cactus that dotted the otherwise barren earth. One of the men passed within two yards of the clump in which Hahksle lay in a nest of small boulders that camouflaged the outline of his body. After the skirmish line had moved on, Hahksle began following it. Early in the afternoon when the men had eaten and were again spread out in their wide-spaced line to search for traces of the non-existent Mohaves, Hahksle dogged his victim until a high rock ledge hid the man momentarily from his companions on either side. Then from a distance of ten yards, the rifle steadied on a boulder, Hahksle shot the soldier in the back.

By the time the rest of the patrol had located the spot where the shot had sounded and gathered around the body of the dead man, Hahksle had vanished. The soldiers searched, but none of them had been on desert station more than a year or two. The Cocopah youth had spent his life learning the desert's ways and had been trained by men whose knowledge of how to hide in the harsh, barren land was distilled from generations of experience. Hahksle did not thank his Paiute mentors, but he used their stratagems. The soldiers ranged far and looked hard, but found no trace of the killer. By the time they returned to the fort carrying the body of their comrade, Hahskle was catching up on his delayed work at the sutler's store.

Because Kahenee stayed to cook supper for the men in the barracks where she worked, she always returned to the settlement later than did her son. It was dusk when she came into the hut, and Hahksle had been sleeping. Her arrival waked him and he sat up, propping himself on an elbow in his blanket-bed on the earthen floor. Kahenee gazed at him steadily for a long moment.

"You killed another *hyko* soldier today." Her words were a flat statement that held no questioning or blame.

"A-ye-ah. I did this thing."

"Then it is over and finished now? He was the other one who came to our house?"

"A-ye-ah. There were two and they are both dead."

Kahenee searched her son's face, found truth in his eyes. She nodded and said, "It is good that it is finished, then."

During the next three weeks while tension in the garrison grew taut and then began to slacken bit by bit, the Cocopahs went about their usual routines. Kahenee made her daily trips to the barracks; she washed shirts, trousers, underwear, and socks. She cleaned the floors, aired the rough blankets on which the soldiers slept, and cooked supper each evening for the company that had hired her. Hahksle's job at the sutler's was less regular. He reported for work each morning, but on some days there was no work to be done and the sutler waved him away. On these days Hahksle returned to the settlement. He carried water from the river to the garden, worked the hard soil between the hills of beans and squash and the rows of maize; he weeded, harvested the ripe vegetables. He was pulverizing an especially stubborn bunch of clods with his wooden shovel-hoe when the soldier rode up.

"Hey, you—Indian!" the man called as he reined in at the edge of the garden plot. "Which one of these shacks does Kootash live in?"

Hahksle did not straighten up at once; the soldier clucked his horse a step closer and raised his voice. "You deaf, Indian? I'm looking for Kootash, the tracker. Captain wants him right away. Where does he live?"

"You will find him there," Hahksle replied, pointing to the hut of the Papago tracker.

With a grunt the soldier spurred his horse ahead. The shortest way to the hut Hahksle had pointed out was through the Cocopah's garden, and the man took it. Hahksle stood looking at the trampled line of crushed bean plants, cracked and broken squash, bent and trampled maize stalks that marked the path the horse had taken through the garden. It took him a moment to reckon up the amount of precious food the soldier had destroyed by his senseless act. As realization grew that the horse had spoiled enough food to sustain him and Kahenee for a week or more, dark anger swept into Hahksle's mind.

His chest heaved as he gulped for air, his head began to throb and ache, and his ears filled with the sounds he had described to Kahenee, a murmur that swelled and grew louder until it became a bubbling roar. Involuntarily he took several steps in pursuit of the mounted soldier, his shovel-hoe upraised to strike. Then the hard-taught lessons of earlier years exercised their discipline. Hahksle stopped short and lowered his shovel-hoe to the ground. With slitted eyes he followed the course of the departing rider. In time, he promised himself, payment would be exacted for the ruined garden. Lips compressed into a thin, hard line, Hahksle forced the anger from him. He turned back to the garden and began trying to salvage some of the trampled food.

It was dark when Kahenee returned, and Hahksle

did not tell her of the incident, but he slept restlessly that night. The next day when his mother asked him about the swath of bare earth that cut through their garden, he shrugged as though it were of no importance.

"A stray horse from the fort. The harm had been done when I got back from the sutler's."

"Did you catch the horse and take it back?"

"Why should I do this thing? It was not my horse. Let whoever the beast belongs to look after it."

Kahenee looked questioningly at Hahksle, but did not question him further.

Now a new series of restless nights came to Hahksle. Almost from the time he lay down to sleep the murmur that grew to a crescendo of roaring filled his head. Even during daylight the sounds sometimes visited him, but when he was awake when they began, he could subdue the sounds before they took full possession of his mind. At night they took him unawares and stole the control he could exert when he was forewarned of their onset. When they came while he slept, he did not awaken until he had already been thrust into a strange and helpless condition that drained him of strength and started body-sweats that left his thin sleeping mat and cotton blankets a soaking tangle.

Though there were many mornings when rising was an effort, Hahksle went daily to the fort. He did not return to the settlement to work in the garden now on the days when the sutler had no jobs for him to do. He set about learning the identity of the soldier who had spoiled the garden. It was not difficult. By watching and listening, he learned that the man was Corporal Biggins, one of the captain's orderlies. He also discovered that Biggins had no fixed hours, no regular duties such as routine patrols or standing sentry, but divided his time between the headquarters building and the barracks occupied by the company to which he was nominally attached.

Hahksle began stalking Biggins. It was a tedious job, requiring great caution because Indians seldom had reason to go into the areas the corporal frequented. Almost two weeks passed before Hahksle could decide on a spot for the ambush; the only place he had any chance of finding Biggins alone was in the latrine back of the barracks in which the corporal was quartered. But even after reaching this decision, Hahksle puzzled for a week over a method by which he could carry out his plan. The latrine was used by the men from two barracks and stood in a barren space between the two buildings. Biggins usually made his visits to it at times when the latrine was being used by other soldiers as well or there were men going toward it or away from it from one of the barracks or the other.

Sanitary arrangements at Fort Mohave were those prescribed by army regulations: the officers' quarters had small individual outhouses, those used by the enlisted men were four-holers. All the outhouses were of flimsy construction, plank walls nailed to a base of heavy timbers with a minimum of framing, so that when it became necessary to move them, a team of mules hitched to their base could skid the buildings to a spot over a freshly dug trench. But the outhouses offered no hiding places. Like most of his people, Hahksle looked on these communal sanitary facilities with disgust. The River People did not void in company with others, but went alone to an isolated spot and covered their excrement quickly, as do cats.

Since the bare area between the two barracks offered

no place to hide, Hahksle used the tops of the buildings. The barracks had been constructed by the Papagos who came from Tucson with the first contingent of
soldiers and followed the Spanish style of building.
They had thick walls of adobe bricks topped by *vigas*—large beams that ran across the narrow structures
and stuck out three or four feet beyond the walls. The
vigas supported the roof, a ceiling of long twigs inter-
woven and topped by a thick layer of sod. To anchor
the *vigas* in place and to keep the earth from washing
off the roof, the exterior walls were built up several
feet above the cottonwood logs from which the beams
were made.

At night Hahksle scooped out a small niche at waist
level in the soft adobe back wall of Biggins's barracks.
With a short run and a jump, one foot in the toehold
created by the niche, he could reach a *viga* and lever
himself to the roof where he could lie without being
seen from below, concealed by the parapet of the wall.
It was a satisfactory hiding place, but a risky one to get
to. Day after day Hahksle risked being seen during the
few moments it took him to scale the wall.

Nearly a month of watchful days passed before the
opportunity he sought arrived. Hahksle had taken his
place on the roof before daybreak and shortly before
sunrise saw Biggins hurry from the barracks into the
unoccupied latrine. Reveille had not yet sounded, the
men were for the most part still in their bunks, and the
barracks area was deserted. Hahksle dropped over the
wall to a *viga*, gripped the beam and slid off it, hung
by his hands barely long enough to check his descent,
and dropped to the ground. He ran to the latrine, knife
in hand. Before Biggins could call or cry out, Hahksle
had slashed the corporal's throat. Still unseen, except

by this dying victim, he walked unhurriedly to the sutler's and reported for work. When the alarm sounded from the barracks area, Hahksle was busy sweeping the floor.

Chapter
9

"We didn't ask the governor to send any help, Swan," Captain Armstrong told the lean, rangy young man with the flared hawk-nose and firm, thin lips who sat across from him in the office. "Fort Mohave can look after its own men."

"Don't take it personal, Captain," Swan said mildly. "Me being sent here's got nothing to do with your soldiers getting killed. I just said what I did about them to make a point."

"Which is?" Armstrong's tone was defensive.

"Which is that you got enough on your hands, so the governor thought you'd be glad to ease up on part of your job, looking after civilians. Anyhow, when he asked me how I'd like to leave the Arizona Rangers and sign on as a deputy U.S. marshal, he mentioned this part of the Territory as being one that needed civilian law."

"Why? There's been no lawlessness here. It's not like it is along the Hassayampa. Or I suppose that part of the Territory's still pretty wild and rough. It was the last time I heard."

"It's getting tamed down," Swan said. "Fact is, the governor feels like he's put too many men there. Now he's trying to cover places where there's fresh prospecting going on and new towns like that one upriver from the fort here—Vadito, where the ferry is. It's growing pretty good, I hear. Must be all of thirty families there now."

"Twenty-seven," Armstrong said. "Not counting Mexicans and Indians, of course."

"And not counting prospectors who don't live any-place. How many would you say have gone up into the Black Mountains and the Hualapais this past year or so?"

Armstrong shook his head. "We can't keep track of the prospectors, Swan. They move around too much. At a guess I'd say there were only two or three claims being worked when the fort was reactivated in '61. Now, still guessing, there are probably a hundred claims being worked within fifty miles of us."

"You've got a special problem here, too, the gover-nor says." Swan held up a hand to stop what was obvi-ously going to be an angry retort from the captain. "No, I don't mean your mysterious killer. I'm talking about the way the folks at Vadito feel about the Army. The governor says that going by the letters he's been getting, if Indian trouble was to break out, your sol-diers couldn't count on getting much civilian help."

"Don't blame me and my men for that," Armstrong bristled. "That goes back a few years, and it's not my fault the contingent that came in from the Presidio made the mistake of requisitioning civilian houses. Even if civilians didn't have title to the land they built on, the people who got moved out were well paid. Of course, those who'd just moved into houses the Army'd built originally were moved out without much warning."

"It still made 'em mad enough to move six or eight miles upriver and build a whole new town," Swan ob-served. "Took the ferry along, too, didn't they?"

Armstrong said stiffly, "That's their privilege."

"Oh, it's no business of mine, Captain," Swan said. "Thing is, they've been sending letters to Prescott asking the governor who's going to protect them from this killer who's running loose."

"They've asked me the same thing," Armstrong retorted curtly. "I tell them we're just as concerned about protecting them as we are about our own men."

"If you don't mind my saying so, they don't seem to think you've done too good keeping your soldiers safe. Three of them killed, now—"

"Four," the captain interrupted in an uncomfortable voice. In response to Swan's questioning look he explained, "You wouldn't have gotten the news before you left Prescott, of course. It only happened three days ago. Corporal Biggins, one of my orderlies. Good man, Biggins—I hate to lose him."

"He was killed the same way the others were?"

"I suppose you'd call it the same. Ambushed, but not in the open as the others were. Had his throat cut right here in the fort, in a latrine."

"No signs your trackers could pick up?"

"They tried, but you know how the ground gets tracked up and packed down hard in a barracks area." Much of the antagonism that had been in Armstrong's voice when Swan first came in was evaporating. "It's obvious what's happening, of course."

"What's that?"

"Why, the killer's a Mohave out to get revenge on the Army for the beatings we've given them."

"Just when did you have a brush with the Mohaves last, Captain?" Swan asked.

"Oh—I suppose the last one you could call a real action was just before we got orders to discontinue regular patrols on the emigrant trails."

"If I remember rightly, that was nearly two years ago, Captain Armstrong. I was with the Arizona Rangers then, and there was talk of us taking over the patrol job, but we didn't have the men to handle it." Swan shook his head. "I just don't see a Mohave waiting so long for his revenge." In afterthought he asked, "The men that were killed, were they scalped?"

"No. But the killer would know he didn't have time to do a Mohave-style scalping. You know their way, they take off the ears and everything above the eyebrows when they scalp a man."

Swan said dryly, "I've seen their work. And one reason I don't figure your killer's a Mohave is because they don't count an enemy dead until they've lifted his scalp. Maybe your mysterious killer's a Paiute."

"Hell, it could be. As far as that goes, it could be anybody."

"Including one of your own men working off grudges. But I guess you've thought about that."

"Of course I have. After the third killing I checked where every man in the garrison was at the time, and they all came up clear."

"That little bunch of Indian huts I saw south of the fort when I rode in, you've checked them?"

"They're all good Indians, Swan. Mostly Papagos who came up in '58 with the detachment that built the fort. Oh, I had the men prowl around out there and ask some questions, but they didn't turn up anything. Not that I thought they would."

"Well." Swan frowned thoughtfully. "You've covered pretty much the same ground I would've if I'd been starting to look for the killer. But I'll nose around on my own after I get settled down."

"I'm afraid we don't have any quarters available, if you're—"

Swan broke in. "I wasn't planning to ask you, Captain. My orders are to set up a station in Vadito. Maybe you can tell me where I can find some kind of shakedown there?"

"Try the ferryman, Hadley's his name. I'm told his wife rents out rooms."

"I'll do that. I guess we understand each other, don't we? I'm not out to step on your toes or mix into Army business, but you're going to see me around the fort here, asking your men questions and poking into this thing until that murder's been hung up."

"Nobody'll be better pleased to see that happen. And I'll give you whatever help I can within reasonable limits."

It was late afternoon when Hank Swan arrived in Vadito, thirty or forty houses that looked down on the Colorado from the bluff above high water mark on which they stood. A few of the dwellings were built of flat, orange-red stones laid in irregular tiers, held together and made weatherproof by a thick plastering of adobe mud. Most of the houses were adobe, though, and all of them straggled face-to-face in a winding double line on either side of the rutted road, little more than a set of tracks, that led through a cut in the bluff down to the ferry landing. In addition to the houses along the road there was a scattering of others set apart from it, small houses that huddled close together as though for mutual protection. Although Swan knew the town was only a few years old, it gave the impression of having been standing there forever, the adobe and fieldstone of the buildings harmonizing with and echoing the tones of the barren earth on which they rested.

Hadley, the ferryman, was in the shabby little saloon that stood at the edge of the bluff where the road dipped through a wagon-wide cut and ran down to the end of the ferry landing. He told Swan after they'd swapped names and the new deputy marshal had explained his business, "Spend more time waiting than I do ferrying these days. But things'll change soon as the Rebs give up and the wagons begin rolling outa the East agin. Now, you say you want a place to stay, well, just go back up the road to the third house on your right and talk to my missus. She's been getting sorta feisty lately about a vacant room we got, so she'll be right glad to see you."

When Swan identified himself and explained his needs to the ferryman's tall, angular wife, she raised her arms and rolled her eyes upward. "Well, mercy be praised! Them government rascals in Prescott finally got around to sending us somebody who'll protect us from Gato!"

"Gato?" Swan frowned, puzzled.

"Why, that's what the Mexicans have named the murdering fiend that's ravishing the countryside. I guess they figure it fits him because from what I hear, it seems like he moves quiet and disappears quick, the way cats do. So most of us just picked the name up. Seems like it's not quite so upsetting if you say 'Gato' instead of just keep calling him 'the killer.' Well, I hope you'll be satisfied with the room I've got for rent, Marshal, because I must say I'll feel a lot safer with you in the house at night."

Swan wasted no time settling into the small but scrupulously clean room that Mrs. Hadley showed him. His moving in consisted of tossing his saddlebags in a corner and sitting down on the side of the narrow bed that almost filled the room and bouncing up and down a time or two, testing the resiliency of its cornhusk-stuffed mattress. Then he strolled around Vadito, the town coming to life as the day's heat diminished. He stopped on the street and introduced himself to those he met and knocked on the doors of a number of houses to get acquainted with their occupants.

In spite of the letters, divided almost equally between anger and worry, that had been received by the governor in Prescott, Swan found most of Vadito's citizens calm and unruffled by the thought that a mysterious killer was roaming around in the vicinity. It took him only a day or two to meet virtually all Vadito's inhabitants, even including the Mexicans and Indians who lived in the cluster of *jacales* apart from the homes of the white settlers. Then during the following days Swan spent his daylight hours riding over the countryside, smelling out the isolated springs and the water-holding rock basins that were the nuclei of tiny oases of green in the raw, arid landscape. He followed faint trails beaten by boots or by the hooves of burros that led to lonely mining claims where prospectors were extracting gold from the veins they'd discovered.

He took the calculated risk of staying away from Fort Mohave. Anxious as he was to question the soldiers of the garrison and the Indians in the adjoining settlement, Swan did not want to disturb the tenuous relationship he'd established with Captain Armstrong by appearing too eager to intrude on Army territory. It wouldn't have made any difference one way or the other, he later consoled himself by thinking, when less than a week after he'd arrived in Vadito, an Army patrol brought in Gato's latest victim.

Dusk was creeping in fast, and Swan had returned only a short time earlier from one of his long rides of exploration. He'd washed off the desert dust and was standing in front of the washstand, shaving, when Hadley rushed home with news of the patrol's arrival.

"Figured you oughta know right away, Marshal," he panted. "They got him down at the saloon now, but soon as they can get the loan of a wagon and team, they're going to take him to the fort, see if the doctor can save him."

Swan put down his razor and began wiping the lather off his face, ignoring the side he hadn't yet shaved. "You mean the soldier's not dead yet?"

"No, he ain't dead, but he ain't far from it. And he ain't a soldier. Prospector, name of Pete Snelson. He works a claim about ten miles north of here." Hadley stopped short, gaping. "Godamitey! That didn't occur to me before. All the others Gato killed was soldiers, wasn't they?"

"That's right." Swan was buckling on his gunbelt. "Thanks for bringing me the news, Hadley. Let's go see what Snelson can tell us."

They found the soldiers of the patrol lined up at the bar, and after a quick glance Swan decided he didn't blame them. They were a tired bunch of men, the dust on their faces striped with white bands where sweat had washed through it, their uniforms stiff and dirt-caked. The wounded prospector lay on the floor, still on the litter the soldiers had improvised to carry him to Vadito. A cumbersome, blood-soaked bandage swathed the man's head. His eyes were closed, his breathing shallow and irregular.

Swan knelt beside the litter. "Snelson! Can you hear me?" The man gave no sign that he'd heard, and even when the marshal grasped his shoulder and shook him gently, the prospector remained comatose.

"I don't think there's much chance he'll come to, Marshal," one of the soldiers said. He'd left the bar and walked over to the litter when Swan first arrived; now he kneeled beside the marshal. "Not unless the doctor can bring him around when we get to the fort. His head's a mess, battered real bad."

"Could he talk when you found him?"

"Barely. He mumbled enough so we could understand it was a lone Indian who'd jumped him."

"Did you try giving him a shot of whiskey?"

"Now, Marshal, you know it's against regulations for us to carry liquor when we're out on patrol. We swabbed his face with water, but that didn't help much. All we could think of was to bandage his head as best we could and bring him back."

Swan called across the room to the saloonkeeper, "Tom! Bring me a big shot of whiskey or brandy in a water glass!"

Snelson was totally limp. His head lolled back as Swan tried to lift him up. The soldier had to help, and between them they dribbled liquor through the prospector's lax lips until the man's mouth filled and he swallowed involuntarily.

"Let that hit bottom and we'll give him another sip," Swan told the soldier. Then he asked, "What made you men decide it was this mysterious killer Indian they call Gato who jumped Snelson? Nobody I've heard about has ever seen Gato."

"Stands to reason, Marshal. Snelson mumbled something about an Indian being to blame, and it's not likely there's more than one Indian killer running loose."

Swan had not taken his eyes off the wounded prospector. The man's eyelids twitched and his lips began to move. "Help me raise him up again," Swan told the soldier. "Let's give him a little more of this whiskey."

Within a few minutes the liquor began to take effect. Snelson stirred; his eyes opened and slowly focused on the men bending over him. His voice thread-thin, he asked the soldier, "Did you get him?"

"Get who?"

"That damn crazy Indian that jumped me."

"Snelson," Swan said urgently, "tell us what happened."

"Not much to tell. I was up at my spring, opening the flume to let water down to my sluice box and I see this Indian standin' there watchin' me. Didn't take him for a redskin right off—he was dressed civilized, shirt and pants and all. Figured him for a Mescin."

"But what did he do? Why did he attack you?" Swan asked.

Snelson's voice rasped in his throat as he replied. "He was holdin' a water gourd, wanted to fill it up outa my spring. Damn it, that water's mine, I need every drop of it to run my sluice, can't waste none on dirty redskins. I told him to git, find him water someplace else, stay off of my claim. Hell, Indians, they always know where to find water."

As he talked the prospector's voice grew steadily weaker. Swan held the glass to the man's lips again, and Snelson drank the rest of the whiskey, swallowing in small gagging gulps.

"Had you ever seen the Indian before?" the marshal asked.

"Not as I know. Never seen anybody look as wild and crazy as he did. Eyes all red and shiny."

"You told him to leave. Then what?"

"He jumped me, the bastard did! Grabbed my shovel away from me and begun swingin'. Taken me by surprise, but I fought him back as best I could."

"Would you know him again if you saw him?"

"Mister, I'll never forget him! And he's marked. I ripped one of his shirt sleeves off while we was fightin' and seen this long jaggedy scar on his lower arm. Looks just like a lightnin' bolt. Sure I'd know him."

Swan heard the soldier kneeling beside him mutter, "Oh, my God!"

"What's the matter?" the marshal asked. "You know something about this Indian Snelson described?"

"I—I'm not sure, Marshal. It might be—"

Before the soldier could say more, Snelson began to twitch and moan, rasping, harsh groans that came from deep inside his chest. The jerking of his body increased in tempo until the prospector gave a convulsive gulp and lay still. Swan spread his palm flat on the man's chest, feeling for a heartbeat.

"Is he dead?" the soldier asked.

"No. His heart's still pumping. But it's pretty weak."

From the doorway a voice called, "Where's the soldier wanted a wagon and team? I got one outside."

"All right, men!" the corporal commanded. "Let's step lively now, get that litter on the wagon."

Almost in unison everyone in the saloon started moving toward the door. Four of the soldiers picked up the litter; the others hurried outside. The man with whom Swan had been talking started to join his companions, but the marshal grabbed his arm.

"Wait a minute, soldier. I want to hear whatever you can tell me about that Indian."

"I'm not sure I can tell you anything. And I've got to go with the squad. Listen, come to the fort. Maybe I'll have something to tell you later."

"Fair enough. What's your name and outfit?"

"Darnell. B Company."

Swan followed the soldier outside and stood watching as the loaded wagon turned in the rutted street and began its journey to Fort Mohave.

Chapter
10

While he was still three or four miles from Fort Mohave the next morning, Hank Swan saw the threads of smoke. They rose into the clean, clear air, etched against the strangely white sky that follows sunrise in the desert, looking like the path a child's dirty outspread fingers make when dragged down a clear windowpane. Though he'd told himself the night before that he'd gain nothing and lose a night's needed sleep if he followed the wagon to the fort, Swan began to feel uneasy. He urged his horse to a faster pace.

By the time he reached the rim of the long gentle slope that led to the fort and could see the source of the smoke threads, they'd dissipated and become part of a long, thin, flat gray cloud that hung low in the windless sky. Below the cloud lay the remains of the Indian settlement that had straggled along the riverbank south of the garrison. Charred circles marked the places where reed huts had stood; squares and rectangles of green identified the bedraggled, trampled remains of the Indians' garden plots. Within the small devastated area nothing moved.

Captain Armstrong sat slumped at his desk in the commandant's office. His face was drawn and tired under an overnight stubble of beard, his eyes bloodshot and watery.

"How'd you get word of the trouble so quick?" he asked Swan.

"You mean the fire? I didn't hear about it. First I knew anything had happened was when I was riding in, saw the smoke. I was on my way here because I've got to talk to Snelson, that prospector one of your patrols brought in last night, and to ask one of your men a few questions."

"Snelson's dead," Armstrong said. "Died in the wagon before it got more than a few miles out of Vadito."

"I was afraid he wasn't going to last long," Swan said. "He was pretty far gone when they left. Well, then, with your permission, Captain, I'll settle for talking to the soldier. His name's Darnell, he's in B Company."

Armstrong gazed at Swan for a moment and replied in a flat voice, "Darnell's dead, too." When Swan's jaw dropped, the captain went on, "You'd better sit down, Marshal. I imagine you'll want to hear the whole story, and it'll take a little time to tell it. I've spent most of the night piecing it together, but there are still a few blanks in it. If I go over it for you, maybe writing my report will be a little easier."

Armstrong had been notified when the squad from B Company was overdue in returning from what should have been an eventless, routine patrol. There wasn't any action indicated when he got the report, and the squad had reported in before he'd thought it necessary to send out a search party. The corporal had made a verbal report of the attack on Snelson and the prospector's death, and Armstrong had jotted down a memo covering the incident, then gone to bed.

"All my people were back safely," he told Swan. "The prospector was dead, and as far as I knew, there weren't any loose ends that needed to be tied up. Hell didn't start popping until sometime after midnight."

Almost immediately after the B Company patrol was dismissed, Armstrong told Swan, Darnell had hurried to the Indian settlement, not even taking time to eat supper. He'd told one of his friends in the company that he needed to check on something the dead prospector had told him and that he'd be back in an hour or so. When Darnell didn't return before the 'lights out' bugle, and after an hour or so passed and he still didn't show up, the soldier to whom he'd mentioned his destination began to worry. He'd gone to the B Company top sergeant, and after the sergeant satisfied himself that Darnell's purpose wasn't just a clandestine visit to an Indian woman, he had taken a couple of men and headed for the settlement.

Since the men didn't know which of the huts Darnell had gone to visit, they'd simply started at the side of the settlement nearest the fort and moved from one dwelling to the next. They'd finally come to the hut, its occupants gone, in which they found Darnell's body sprawled in a pool of congealed blood from the knife slash that had almost taken off his head.

"Who'd been living in the hut?" Swan asked.

"Damn it, nobody seems to know!" Armstrong snapped angrily. "The sergeant who'd gone looking for Darnell—and he won't be a sergeant by noon today, I promise you—didn't use his head. He should have left Darnell lying there and come back to report the murder to me. Instead he had the men with him carry the body to the dispensary, right through the garrison area, even though he could see the surgeon wasn't going to be able to help."

One of the sentries had seen the B Company contingent carrying the corpse into the garrison and called

the sergeant of the guard. The sergeant had roused the
officer of the day, who'd sent for his orderly.

"God knows," Armstrong told Swan feelingly, "latrine rumors can sweep through a post this size in just
a few minutes, and Darnell's killing wasn't just a
rumor, it was a fact."

All the activity generated by the sentry calling out
the guard sergeant had somehow trickled from one
barracks to the others in a matter of minutes. The officers and men were edgy anyhow because of the earlier killings, and within a whisper of time after news of
Darnell's death began circulating, it was followed by
the rumor that the murderer was hiding in one of the
huts in the Indian settlement. Before the officers could
reach their commands, the cry arose, "Burn the redskins out!" and men carrying torches were running
toward the settlement, ignoring commands of the noncoms who tried to stop them. There were few noncoms
who made the effort; most of them joined the men in
the burning that followed.

Armstrong, asleep in his quarters, hadn't been
roused by the officer of the day until after the first huts
were blazing.

"By then it was too late to do anything," he told
Swan bitterly. "Before I could get there, the whole settlement was on fire and the Indians were running for
their lives."

"How many of them were killed?"

"I haven't had a report of any casualties yet. There
wasn't a lot of shooting, though. Most of the men had
their minds set on burning and left their rifles behind."

"I guess you did have somebody check out what was
left of the hut where Darnell was found to see if there
was anything that might give us a lead to who was living in it?"

"Yes. But there wasn't anything left of it. Ashes. A few pieces of broken pots, nothing else."

Swan frowned thoughtfully. "I can just about guess, now, what was on Darnell's mind last night when I was talking to him in Vadito. We'd got a little whiskey into Snelson, and he could talk a little bit. Darnell was helping me, and when Snelson mentioned that the Indian who jumped him had a long, jagged scar like a bolt of lightning on one arm, I think Darnell recognized that scar. It must've been on some Indian he knew about."

"Darnell had the reputation of being an Indian-lover if that's worth anything to you. I found out last night when I was trying to get to the bottom of things that Darnell was always after the Papago scouts, wanting them to teach him their language, things like that."

"It might've helped if I'd known it last night. Doesn't do me much good now, him being dead and all the Papagos gone."

"I hope some of them will be back during the day. They ran south along the river, and I sent detachments out at daybreak to try to catch up with them, find them, get them to come back to the fort."

Swan stood up, hitched his gunbelt into a more comfortable position. "I guess I'll be riding south myself, Captain. There's not much I can do here. You don't want my help or need it to settle your men down. When I come back, I'll want to talk to a few of them, especially men in B Company, see if any of them recall hearing Darnell say anything that might be useful. But I'd say your killer ran before the other Indians stampeded. My best bet's to follow your scouts, see if I can talk to any Indians they might've caught up with."

Armstrong hesitated, then made the difficult request. "If you do learn anything, Marshal, I'll appreciate you passing it on to me. Anything I can put in my report that'll make this mess look better will be a help."

Swan nodded. "Don't worry. I can't see it'd do either of us any good to sit on information. I'll pass anything I learn on to you, and I'm sure you'll do the same thing."

Riding out of Fort Mohave, Swan had no other plan than to follow the river south for a few miles. He reasoned that the fleeing Indians couldn't have covered much ground in the few hours that had passed since the settlement was burned. Darkness must have slowed them initially—there were women and children with the group—and he could move faster on horseback than the Indians could on foot.

After a fruitless morning of crisscrossing a strip some two miles wide along the Colorado's bank Swan began to question both the logic of his reasoning and the advantage he'd thought a horse would give him. He had not seen a single Indian, nor had either of the three scouting patrols from the fort he'd encountered and stopped to compare notes with.

"Beats me where them redskins went," said the sergeant in command of one of the detachments as he mopped his sweaty face and forehead. "You don't figure they might've got across to the other side of the river, do you, Marshal?"

Swan shook his head. "I've been looking, but I'd say there's not a place between here and the fort where it's possible to ford the river. No, they've just scattered. Must be hiding in a cave or something, waiting for dark."

"Captain's gonna be put out, I guess," the sergeant said ruefully. "He told us to turn back at noon whether we catch up with the Indians or not. Just the same, if we don't catch up, he's gonna want to know how come."

"Wish I could help you," Swan sympathized. "I'm as anxious to talk to some of those Indians as the captain is."

As Swan sat watching the patrol move off, the men talking loudly, cursing the heat and the rough country, the thought occurred to him that they were telegraphing their movements so far ahead of themselves that the fleeing Papagos would have no trouble avoiding the patrol unless the Indians were both deaf and blind. Simultaneously he realized that he'd been duplicating the soldiers' mistakes. While his horse gave him the advantages of speed and mobility, it was at the price of silent movement and minimum visibility. He nudged the buckskin's flanks to set it moving again, and though he followed the same pattern of zigzagging between the river and the high mesalands to the east, Swan looked now not only for fleeing Papagos, but for a suitable hidden vantage point.

Within the hour he found a spot that suited his new plan, a deeply corrugated expanse of broken ground at the base of a small butte. Dismounting, he led the horse into the concealment of one of the ravines, dropped the reins over its head so the buckskin would stand, and scrambled up the precipitous twenty-foot slope to the top of the butte. Even from that small height he commanded a view of most of the terrain between butte and river. Selecting a boulder near the butte's edge, Swan sat down in its shadow. The soft gray of his flannel shirt, the faded tan of his duck jeans, merged with the hues of the earth. Leaning back against the rough rock, he set himself to wait.

An hour went by, then another. Though Swan was shielded by the boulder from the sun's direct rays, re-

flected heat from the parched ground enveloped him.
He forced himself to remain motionless, letting the
drops of sweat roll off nose and chin to his soaked
shirt. Twice the buckskin stamped and whinnied, and
Swan risked a soft-voiced word to reassure the animal
that he was still close by. Shortly after the third hour
of his waiting watch began, Swan's patience was re-
warded. His eyes caught a flicker of movement perhaps
two hundred yards distant at the edge of a low mesa
that broke the generally flat sweep of land up from the
riverbed.

An Indian man stepped cautiously from the shadow
cast by the mesa. He was followed by another man,
then by three women, two children, and finally by two
more men. Swan waited until the little band reached
the center of the wide stretch of clear ground that lay
between the mesa and the ravine-cut stretch where his
horse was hidden, then he stood up and hailed the Indians.

"*To-je*! Bean People! Will you listen to a message
from the owl?"

At the sound of Swan's voice the small group of Papagos began to scatter and run, but when the owl was
mentioned, the man leading them barked a sharp command and the others stopped. Almost three centuries
of proselytizing by Spanish friars and U. S. mission-
aries had not weaned the Bean People from their tribal
beliefs. To them the owl was not a harbinger of death
as it was to the Cocopahs. In Papago religion the souls
of their dead entered the bodies of owls, and the owls
that harbored such souls were messengers from the
Keeper Of All Smokes. No Papago dared to ignore a
message brought by an owl, regardless of the interme-
diary who transmitted it.

Facing Swan, the Papago leader called, "Why would

the owl speak to someone who is not of the Bean
People?"

"Because he could find none of them who would listen. All the Bean People were running in fear and had
no time to hear his words."

"Ai-yah. This thing is true," the leader ac-
knowledged. "The soldiers were burning our homes.
We were afraid they would kill us."

Swan improvised. "The owl knows this. Will you listen now to what he said?"

"We will listen."

Quickly the marshal came down from the butte and
walked to the waiting Papagos. He told them, "This is
what the owl said to me. The soldiers have not become
your enemies. They burned your homes because they
were angry and afraid. One of them had been killed in
a house belonging to the Bean People."

"No," the leader said quickly. "The house belonged
to the Cocopahs. The young man and the old woman,
his mother, are the ones who killed the soldier."

"Is the young man the one they call Gato?" Swan
asked.

"We do not know this thing. Soldiers have been
killed, and some say it is one called Gato who did it.
But the Cocopah man is called Hahksle and his mother
is Kahenee. Did the owl not tell you this?"

"I have told you what the owl said. The soldiers are
still your friends. They won't harm you if you go
back."

"We do not want them as friends any more. Our
houses have been burned and we do not want to go
back. We will go to our own country and live with our
own people again."

"If that is what you want to do, that is what you
should do," Swan said. "But before you go, tell me

something in return for my gift to you of the owl's message."

"What is the thing you ask us to tell you?"

"All you know about the Cocopahs who were living among you."

"We know little of them. They were fighting some Mohaves one day when the soldiers found them and helped them kill the Mohaves. The soldiers brought the Cocopahs to the fort. Our people gave them food and helped them as we could. They lived beside us. What more is there that we can tell you?"

"From which Cocopah village did they come?" Swan asked.

"They did not tell us. They said they had been captured by the Paiutes and taken far to the north by them. They had escaped from the Paiutes and were going to join their own people when the Mohaves attacked them. It is not a long time since they came to our village, we know nothing more than this."

"Where are they now?"

"We do not know. We do not know that the young man is the one who is called Gato. If he killed anybody, we do not know about it."

"And none of you saw them leave their house after the soldier was killed there? You cannot tell me which way they travelled?"

"We did not see them. We do not know. Perhaps they went back north, to the *quiqusqu*, to live again with the Paiutes. How could we know such things as these you ask us?"

"I guess you wouldn't, at that," Swan said, more to himself than to the Papagos.

There was a moment of silence, then the Indian leader said, "We have answered your questions, and you have given us the message from the owl. Now we will go where we have started, back to our own land."

Swan made no effort to stop the Papagos and wasted no words in trying to persuade them to return to the fort. He stood watching as the little group filed past him and continued their long journey southward. Walking slowly back to his horse, he swung into the saddle and rode off in the opposite direction to that taken by the Indians. He was not satisfied, but at least he'd learned things he hadn't known before. Gato's identity was no longer a total mystery, and somewhere in the vicinity of Fort Mohave, Swan told himself, he'd be able to pick up the trail that would lead him to the killer.

Chapter
11

"Now, damn it, Captain! That man of yours, Darnell, he must've told somebody why he went to talk to those two Cocopahs!"

"If he did, I haven't been able to find them," Armstrong told Swan. "Darnell wasn't like most enlisted men, Marshal. He didn't mix the way other soldiers do. For one thing he was educated. I told him several times he was officer material, but he'd just laugh and shake his head. I promoted him to corporal once, but he got into a scrape and I had to take his rank away from him. I think now that's what he wanted me to do."

"And he didn't have any close friends?"

"None I can turn up. He got along pretty well with everybody, but he wasn't especially friendly with anybody."

Swan rubbed his chin. "Well, I'm not sure he'd've been able to tell me anything more than I know already. But I'd've given a lot to've talked to him on the chance he could."

"I think this Gato's gone for good, Marshal," Armstrong said. "I know I'm not going to take any chances, though. There'll be no more Indians on this post, as long as I have anything to say about it. When my men are patrolling they'll be doing it two by two,

no more single sentries, and no more breaking up
squads when there's field work being done."

"You don't sound so sure we've really seen the last
of him," Swan observed.

"Whether we have or not, I'll take no risks,"
Armstrong replied stiffly.

"You're not pulling in your patrols, though?" Swan
frowned. "I can't cover all the places where there are
one or two prospectors working a digging."

"We'll still go patrolling," the captain promised.
"We just won't lose any more men."

Swan hadn't really believed that Captain Armstrong's men were going to be as careful as their
commander intended for them to be, but as weeks went
by and there were no more soldiers killed, he began to
change his mind. The unknown murderer was still in
the vicinity, of that the marshal had proof. The killings
didn't stop. A pair of prospectors coming in to Vadito
for supplies found the first body on a faint trail four
miles from the settlement. The dead man had been a
prospector himself, bound on the same errand, and
when Swan dug out the bullet that had ended the
man's life, it was an Army issue .45-.70.

Almost a month went by, and people in the little
town as well as the men at the fort were beginning to
breathe easier. Then the next sign of Gato's work was
discovered by an Army patrol making a sweep around
the diggings that were scattered over a twenty-mile area
centered on the fort. This time there were two victims.
Both were prospectors, partners, who'd camped on
Sacramento Wash between the Black Mountains and
the Hulapais. Swan didn't get to see the bodies—the
patrol buried them—but the descriptions he got from
the men who were there left little doubt that Gato had
been responsible.

By now the marshal had formed a reasonably clear picture of the pattern Gato followed. The thing that stood out most clearly in Swan's mind was that the Cocopah killed but didn't rob. The only items he'd stolen from the beginning of his murders had been the guns and ammunition boxes from his first soldier victims. The next thing that had impressed Swan was that Gato so far had killed only soldiers and prospectors. The third item was that in all except the case of one soldier Gato had been virtually face-to-face with each of the men he'd slain.

It was a slim pattern at best, but it stood up under Swan's testing well enough to cause him to file it away in his mind and carry it there through the long period that followed, when Gato disappeared into the desert for several months. Then, the pattern surfaced unbidden and led him to question the story of the teamster who rattled into Vadito late one afternoon claiming that a crazy-looking Indian had waylaid and robbed him and his two companions and killed the other men. He had the bodies in the otherwise empty wagon to prove his story.

"Where were you coming from when this happened?" Swan asked. There was something about the teamster's account that didn't sound quite right.

"From the Denbow Mine on Lone Peak. We'd hauled a load of star drills and jackhammers and mercury there from Prescott. Finish unloading too late to start back last night, stayed in the bunkhouse."

"How come you didn't go back to Prescott if that's where you're from?"

"Marshal, thats one hell of a road and we didn't much cotton to going over it again. We got to talking with the men at Denbow's—they just about talked us into going on out to California. We was on the way to the ferry when that wild Indian jumped us. It must've been the one they call Gato."

"How'd he miss killing you?" Swan asked.

"I was on the other side of the wagon from him. I jumped off and took out. He shot at me once, but missed. After a while, when it got quiet, I went back to the wagon. My partners were dead, and he'd robbed their bodies."

Swan said nothing, but walked over to the wagon and took a close second look at the bodies. Both men had been shot through the head, and the right cheeks of both were peppered with powder burns. He came back to the teamster and indicated the pistol that hung from a holster at the teamster's waist.

"Did you say you traded shots with the Indian?"

"No, sir! I didn't stop to draw down on him. All I wanted was to get clear!"

"Mind if I look at your gun?"

"Help yourself," the man said.

He slipped the revolver out of its holster and handed it over. Swan levered out the cylinder pivot pin and inspected the percussion caps on each side of the chambers. Three of them were dull, but the copper cases of the other two shone brightly.

"You might as well stop lying," Swan told him. "There wasn't any Indian, was there? You heard about Gato at the mine, and it gave you an idea. Then you shot your friends and took their money. I expect you got paid for the load you dropped at Denbow's, didn't you? And I expect you were the one who wanted to take the money and go to California. Only your partners weren't as crooked as you."

Very little prodding was required after that. The surprised teamster caved in after a half-dozen questions convinced him that Swan must have witnessed the kill-ings himself.

"There's going to be others like him, too," the mar-shal told Captain Armstrong a few days later. "Some prospector's going to get greedy and backshoot his part-ner and claim it was Gato. And every time some poor desert rat miscalculates on how far he can go without finding a fresh water hole, whoever finds him dead on the *malpais* will swear Gato killed him even if there's not a mark on him."

"You could be right," Armstrong agreed. After Swan had shown that he wasn't out to step on military toes or assert civilian over Army authority, the com-mandant of Fort Mohave had dropped his original prickliness. "But this new killing you're going south to find out about, you're pretty sure Gato's responsible?"

Swan nodded. "Looks like it from the story I got. Emigrant couple heading west, stopped for a day or two at the Hanson Tanks. There was only one other family there, and they pulled out on the same day. That evening the woman was in the wagon and heard a shot at the tank. Her husband was there filling a bucket. She thought maybe he'd shot a snake. Looked out and saw this Indian running off and her husband shot."

"Did the Indian look like Gato?" Armstrong asked.

"Hell, who knows what Gato really looks like? The only one who's lived long enough to tell us anything was that first prospector he killed, and that's nearly a year ago. Too bad your men didn't pay more attention to him when he was working around the fort."

"One Indian looked pretty much like the next to most of them before this Gato business started," Armstrong said. "Well, I'll hear from you when you get back, I guess?"

"Sure. Only don't look for me right away. My hunch is that Gato's moving this time. If I pick up a trail, I'll follow it. I'd say he's heading for the Mohaves or Buckskins, maybe even for the Chemehuevis. Anyhow, I expect I'll go on to the Bill Williams River as long as I'm so close to it. Most emigrant wagons stop there, and I'll spread the word among 'em to be careful, ask 'em to pass it along to whoever they meet."

Emigrants had never been numerous on the Mormon Trail that branched off the Santa Fe Trail and struck southwest through the middle of Arizona Territory. Most of the wagons heading for California followed the old Mission Trail along the Gila River. The few emigrants who were in a hurry and braved the nearly waterless desert had to depend on almost nonexistent springs and the few tanks that were dotted through the sunbaked *malpais*. The tanks were rock or hardpan formations that caught rain runoff. The water in them was likely to be covered with a scum of green algae and might also hold the bloated body of a small desert animal or two. It was wet, though, and staved off dehydration in humans and animals, and most travellers stopped when they reached one.

Hank Swan found only two or three emigrant wagons at the half-dozen tanks he visited as he rode south trying to pick up Gato's trail. It wasn't until he reached the Bill Williams River that he encountered a sizeable concentration of wagons, nine of them. Six were drawn together in a half-circle; one stood a littlje apart upstream; the other pair was at a distance from the semi-circle on the downstream bank. There were people around the large group of wagons, and Swan stopped and dismounted beside them. They were, he learned, a party of families who'd abandoned the war-ravaged South and were heading for California. They'd learned the desert was kinder to travellers by night and were just getting ready to pull out. They'd make their ten or fifteen miles and stop again at dawn, sleep through the heat of the day, and move on again an hour or so before sunset.

Swan visited with them while they completed their preparations to leave and asked them to pass on the caution he'd given them about Gato to any travellers they met coming east. He stood by the river and watched the little train as it pushed off, then led the buckskin to the single wagon. This, he discovered, belonged to a middle-aged couple who'd found California's golden promise to be illusory and were going back home to Texas. The thought that they might be in danger made them nervous, and the man spanned his mules and left at once. Swan wished them a good trip and headed for the two wagons that remained. A girl, he guessed her age as being about ten, sat on the seat of one of them. She wore a blue gingham dress and sunbonnet and was cradling a doll with flowing blond hair.

"Shh!" she put her fingers to her lips and whispered as Swan approached, "Mama and Papa are asleep inside."

He dropped his voice to match her whisper. "All right. If they didn't get waked up by all the noise that's been made by the other wagons, I wouldn't want to rouse them. What's your name, young lady?"

"Nellie. Nellie Bronson. And this is Rosie." She held up the doll for him to admire.

"Well. I'd say Rosie's mighty pretty. He looked at the girl's green eyes, shaded by the brim of the sunbonnet, and added, "But so are you for that matter."

"Thank you. Not as pretty as Rosie, though. I purely love her. Papa sent away for her all the way to

Los Angeles, and she came on the Wells Fargo express wagon to Gila City. That's where we lived when I had my birthday."

"That's where you call home, then?"

"Oh, no. I'm California born. Mama's told me all about how she carried me inside of her all the way around Cape Horn from New York to where we landed in San Francisco, and then on another boat to Sacramento. That's where I was born. Mama stayed there, you see, because it was too rough in the goldfields for her when Papa went back to work on his claim."

There was a stirring behind the drawn canvas flaps of the wagon cover. They parted and a man's head and shoulders pushed between them. His hair was tousled, his eyes heavy-lidded and blinking in the late afternoon brightness.

"Nellie, who're you talking to?" he asked before he saw Swan standing by the wagon. "Who're you, mister? And what d'you want?"

"My name's Swan, Mr.—Bronson, is it? I'm a U.S. marshal."

"Well, you're not looking for me. I haven't broken any laws I know about."

Bronson crawled out and sat beside Nellie. He was a big man, Swan saw, wide-shouldered and deep-chested. The biceps that bulged under his balbriggan underwear belonged to a man used to hard work. Over the underwear he wore the Levi's blue denim jeans that had become a virtual uniform for miners and prospectors. Bronson's hair was dark with a threading of gray beginning to show at the temples. His eyes were light brown, his brows heavy. His jaw was heavy, too, and needed shaving. He rubbed the sleep out of his eyes with a hand that had thick, callused fingers.

"Are you after somebody, Swan?" he asked. "Because if this is just a friendly visit, I'll ask you to come back later on after I've had my sleep out." He glanced along the riverbank, shook his head. "Or maybe I've had it out. It's later than I thought if all the others have gone on."

"You weren't travelling with them, were you?" Swan asked.

"No. We're going north. I heard in Gila City about the new strike up along the Colorado in the Black Mountains."

"I've just come from there. It's where my station is, just south of the Blacks."

"Is that right." Bronson's brows pulled together. "Is it really a good strike or just another wild story?"

"Oh, they're finding gold, all right. But it's not easy."

"None of it's easy. I've learned that." Bronson grinned. "But the easy lodes are worked out fast. I'd as soon take my chances in a place that's not going to bring a rush of greenhorns."

From inside the wagon a woman's voice called. "Ed? Is there something wrong?"

"No, Manda. Go back to sleep. I'll be there in a minute," he replied.

Swan was saying, "I'm sorry, Mr. Bronson, I didn't mean to wake your family," when a woman's head thrust through the flaps.

"Who're you talking to?" she asked. Her startlingly green eyes were partly veiled by strands of deep red hair. She brushed the hair aside, tucking it up, and focused her eyes on Swan.

"This man's a U.S. marshal," Bronson explained. "I haven't found out yet why he woke us up."

"Maybe we'd better talk privately," Swan suggested. "If you'd like to walk a little way with me?"

Bronson frowned at him, then nodded. "Wait'll I slip my feet into my brogans." He crawled back through the canvas flaps and came out almost at once. He'd pulled on calf-high miner's boots, but hadn't laced them. He dropped to the ground and said, "All right. We'll walk a ways."

When they were out of earshot of the woman and girl, Swan told Bronson, "I don't want to get you started worrying, Mr. Bronson, but if you're heading north, I've got to warn you to keep your eyes open every minute of the time."

"Why? Some kind of trouble up that way?"

"One man trouble. There's a killer wandering around, and nobody knows where to look for him next."

"What kind of killer? Who's he killed?"

"Eight or nine men so far. No women, not yet."

"What does he look like?" Bronson asked.

"That's the big trouble. I can't tell you. I've never seen him, neither has anybody else who's still alive."

"What?" Bronson blurted incredulously. "You mean this fellow's murdered eight or nine men, and nobody's ever seen him?"

Swan was slow to answer. Finally he said, "That's about the size of it. One man stayed alive long enough to tell us a little bit. The killer's Indian, more'n likely a Cocopah. He's young and he's got a long, jagged scar on one arm between his wrist and elbow."

"Which arm?"

"That's something else I don't know. About all I can say to you is that you better keep your gun handy and don't let any Indian come close to your wagons. We do know one thing more. Whatever he looks like, this In-

GATO   *129*

dian sneaks up on you like a cat and vanishes like one.
That's why folks who've heard about him gave him the
name he's called by. Gato."

Bronson shook his head. "I just can't figure nobody
ever seeing him. Not if he's done as many killings as
you say."

"Oh, he's done them. Maybe more than we know
about yet. I've got a hunch he's murdered a few lone
prospectors, and their bodies haven't turned up."

"And you don't know where he might be?"

"Not right now. He's sly and tricky. I'm not
ashamed to tell you, Bronson, he's had me flopping
like a turkey just off the chopping block for damned
near a year running after him."

"You've never caught up with him at all?"

"Never come close. But I'll tell you this, and it
might ease your mind some. He headed south after his
last killing at the Hanson Tanks. That's a good ways
north of here, about 80 miles. I trailed him from there
a ways, and I'd guess he's holed up someplace in the
Chemehuevis. That's where I lost him."

"You're not sure, though?"

"I'm sure of where his trail faded out. But I can't
guarantee he won't double back," Swan said.

Bronson rubbed his chin thoughtfully. "Well, I guess
I'll take my chances on him missing us. I don't like to
turn away from something I start on, Marshal."

"That's up to you. I guess you've thought about
your wife and little girl?"

"I can look after them. I always have." Bronson
shifted his eyes toward the wagons. His wife was bending over a just kindled fire on the riverbank. He said,
"All right, Swan. You've warned me and I thank you.
Now let's just put this Gato aside, and you come have
supper with us. It won't be much, side-meat and spuds,

but I guess it'll taste good to a man who's been trailing by himself."

"If you're sure it won't run you short—"

"It won't. I stocked up good before we left Gila City. Figured on enough to get us to Fort Mohave and a little bit extra. And it'll do us good to visit with you. I'm curious about what it's like up where we're going. I guess Amanda is, too."

Chapter
12

Over supper and drinking coffee beside the dying fire later on, Hank Swan learned a lot about the Bronson family from what they told him, learned much more from what they said to one another, and filled in a few gaps by guesses based on what he'd learned of the prospecting breed of men who followed the promise of gold.

Ed Bronson had gotten wind of the big new strike in Gila City earlier than most of the disheartened remnants of the gold rush miners who were still working California's Mother Lode in 1857. By that time the boom days of the Forty-niners had vanished. Big-scale hydraulic mining was beginning to extract gold at the headwaters of the streams down which the flakes and nuggets had once washed in the spring floods.

Bronson had moved steadily south after Nellie's birth in Sacramento. The gold had given out early in the northern diggings, and he and Amanda and Nellie had followed the rivers and rills along the foothills of the Sierras' western slope. They'd camped briefly or lived uncomfortably in shanties at Dutch Flat, then at Coloma and Fiddletown, Angel's Camp, Sonora and Columbia, Mariposa and Bootjack, and were at Coarsegold on the North Fork of the San Joaquin

River when Ed heard of the new bonanza on the Gila, far south in Arizona Territory.

Nellie hadn't been quite six years old when they left Coarsegold, but she remembered the long stagecoach ride to Los Angeles where they'd stopped briefly while her father assembled an outfit that would carry them across the desert to Arizona. Unlike most prospectors, Bronson kept his poke strings pretty tightly tied, so he had the money to buy two wagons and four mules to team each wagon, together with the food and supplies and the big water casks that were lashed to the wagons to get them across the waterless Mohave desert.

Amanda Bronson drove one wagon, Ed handled the other, and Nellie divided her time between them. They followed the century-old Mission Trail beaten by the Spaniards between California and Arizona, but even with good teams and tight new wagons it'd been a long trip. They'd start before sunrise and travel until midmorning. They'd stop while Ed unhitched the teams and watered them, then all three of them would rest through the hot part of the day in the shade of the wagons. Late in the afternoon they'd start out again and travel until long after dark.

Amanda hadn't liked Gila City at first, but neither had Ed or Nellie. After the wooded foothills of the Mother Lode where it seemed there'd been a singing creek every few yards and a river every mile or so, the raw, sunbaked country along the Gila River looked desolate and unfriendly. The Bronsons had been among the first tiny trickle of goldseekers to arrive there. Gila City, when they'd seen it first, had been a lonely straggle of a couple of dozen tents and wagons along the riverbank. Then the trickle became a flood, and in a year or less the two dozen shelters became two hundred, and in less time than they'd believed, two thousand. A few of the newly rich prospectors had even started building adobe houses.

With the dedicated optimism of the perennial gold-seeker Ed Bronson had told his wife, "When I find a lode, we'll build us a house, Manda."

"Why bother?" Amanda smiled, and Ed saw the smile but missed the veiled bitterness in her voice. "We've lived in tents a lot more than we have in houses. I don't think I'd remember how to sweep a floor or wash windows or make up a real bed with mattresses and springs and sheets instead of blankets."

"Now, Manda, I'm not joking about a house."

"I'm not just joking about the tent." Amanda swept an arm to indicate the bare, sunbaked ground on both sides of the Gila River. "Any lode you find is going to have to be right rich, Ed, to persuade me it's worth living in a place like this the rest of my life."

"Anyplace where you can make a pile fast is a good place to live."

"That's as may be. What about Nellie? She needs to grow up where she can have playmates, a school to go to."

"Seems to me she's gotten along without 'em so far. And you're doing right good, teaching her."

Ed's jaw muscles corded in a way that Amanda recognized only too well, but she was determined not to give in this time.

"Oh, Ed! Look at Nellie. Listen to her talk. She still acts like a baby and she's almost ten years old. I do what I can to teach her grammar and spelling and a few bits and pieces of whatever I can still remember from school. But it's a mortal pity how lonesome she is and how little she can learn here."

"Well, that doll I've ordered for her birthday might be some kind of playmate for her. The rest will just have to wait. I want to stick it out here a while longer, Amanda."

They stuck it out while discouraged prospectors left and hopeful new ones arrived. Ed was luckier than most, or better. He kept finding good placer pockets to pan, but in spite of all the panning he did, along the river and on both sides of it in the short creeks that fed it, he never did find the lode he was seeking.

"I guess there's not any real lode here any more than there was in California," he admitted to Amanda one evening after he'd returned from a week along the river. "And the placer pockets are playing out, too. But I hear they're uncovering some pretty rich ore up north in the Black Mountains and the Hualapais and Eldorados."

"When do you want to leave?" she asked. Amanda had noticed her husband's growing restlessness, had seen the number of tents and wagons on the riverbank diminishing daily, just as she'd seen other settlements fade and vanish in the Mother Lode country.

"Pretty soon, I guess. We're in good shape for money now, but the way things are going, it's getting to be time we moved on. We'll give it another three or four weeks, though."

Ed's three or four weeks stretched into twice that many months, and when they finally left Gila City, the town had shrunk until it was even smaller than when they arrived. There were a dozen wagons and tents left, along with four or five adobes that had been built by those with more hope than judgment.

They headed north along the Colorado. Except that they didn't have to worry about hauling water with them, it was a repetition of their trip from California. Ed handled one wagon, Amanda the other. Nellie alternated from one wagon to another, but now she al-

ways cradled her cherished Rosie in her lap as the
wagons crept north. Even by travel standards of the
1860's it was a slow trip. Ed had turned a profit by
selling one four-mule team in Gila City, so now there
were only two mules on each wagon. Ed's prospecting
slowed them, too. If he saw a formation that looked
promising, he took time to stop and test it. On a lot of
occasions the wagons would stand all day while he
unhitched Jehoshaphat, his riding mule, and went off to
take a close look at some distant ridge that had caught
his eye. Even without Ed's side trips, though, their
progress would have been slow because the country
was so rough and canyon-cut.

Not infrequently they'd lose the better part of a day
travelling along one rim of a canyon, moving at right
angles to the direction they should be taking, looking
for a place where the canyon walls sloped gently
enough for the wagons to descend. Sometimes they'd
be forced to follow the ravines until they threaded
down to ditch-sized gullies that the wagon wheels could
bounce across. Occasionally, encountering a shallow,
wide canyon with steep walls, Ed would have to break
out the block and tackle carried by all experienced
wagon travellers. Then with the ropes snubbed around
the biggest rock spur in the vicinity, the wagons would
be lowered to the canyon floor and hauled up on the
other side.

This, too, was an all-day job. Amanda handled the
mules, double-teamed to the fall-rope, while Ed rode
down in the wagonbed, fending the vehicle off the
jagged wall with a wagon tongue. Even little Nellie had
her part in the operation, which was to set and remove
the wooden blocks that chocked the wagon wheels as
the vehicle inched closer and closer to the rim during
the critical moments before it swung out over the edge.

It was not until they reached the mouth of the Bill Williams River that they saw other travellers. The Bronsons got to the stream during the early hours of a typically bright morning and saw a half-dozen conveyances similar to their own clustered across the stream. Ed, in the lead wagon, started across the wide, sandy delta, but a man came running down from the other wagons and waved him back. Bronson reined in and alighted. Behind him Amanda stopped the second team.

Cupping his hand to his mouth, the stranger had called, "Don't try to ford here, 'tain't safe. Go upriver till you come to a cottonwood grove—that'd be the best place to cross."

Obeying the voice of experience, Ed led the little caravan east, and after a long period of jolting over a boulder-studded trail, they found the ford and crossed without getting the wheelhubs wet. Then they'd turned back west along the riverbank and for at least one evening had enjoyed human companionship—the first they'd had since leaving Gila City almost two months earlier.

By the time the Bronsons had told Hank Swan their family saga and Swan traded a few of his early experiences in the Arizona Rangers in return, the night was well along, the supper fire had died, and the last dregs of coffee in the pot had been drunk. Nellie had gone to sleep on Amanda's lap, still cuddling Rosie, and had long since been taken to the wagon and tucked into bed.

"What's it really like up where we're going?" Amanda asked.

Hank could tell she'd been saving the question, not really wanting to ask it, dreading the answer more than a little bit. He tried to choose his words carefully.

"Well, it's desert mostly. But hills, too. And some valleys with water tucked away here and there. Not many people, but I guess they'll come in time."

"And Hank says they're making good strikes all over those hills," Ed Bronson said. They'd gotten past the formalities and down to first names during the long evening of talk.

"If there's gold to be found, I'm sure you'll find it," Amanda assured her husband.

"How about the road?" Bronson asked.

"You follow the river pretty close, it's been used enough so you won't go wrong. A few bad spots, but they're easy to get around. If you need supplies, the sutler's at the fort can fix you up if you don't mind paying sutler's prices. Not much need to, though. Further on up there's a little town, Vadito. There's a store there."

"And you're sure this—this Gato, you're sure he's left up there and come down close to where we are now?" she asked.

"Pretty sure. Long as Ed keeps watch and has a gun handy, you'll make it without danger," Swan assured them. "Anyhow, I'll be riding on myself tomorrow. I'd ride alongside you if it wasn't that I've got to move faster'n your wagon can and might have to zigzag off the road now and then if I find any signs of Gato. But just keep moving along easy. You'll make it where you're going all right."

Chapter
13

That night after Amanda and he had crawled into the wagon to sleep, Ed asked anxiously, "You're worried about us going on up north, aren't you, Manda?"

"Some. Aren't you after what the marshal said?"

"Maybe a little bit. I figure I can handle one lone, crazy Indian."

"But if he sneaks up—" Amanda began.

Ed broke in. "I'll keep careful watch and I'll shoot any Indian that shows up without waiting to ask him any questions. Don't worry, hon, I'll keep you and Nellie safe."

"Well, you always have. Anyhow, if the marshal's looking for him and he's going north, too—" She stopped, thought a moment, and asked, "But didn't he say this Gato started out up near where we're heading?"

"There's not all that much to worry about, Manda. Look at it this way. If it was a year ago this Indian started up there, he's not likely to go back. He'll know they're looking for him. And hearing about him probably spooked out a few prospectors who were already there and kept a few more away from that part of the Territory. So it ought to give me a pretty clear field. And from what I've heard, there's plenty of real promising formations in those mountains we're heading for."

Amanda spoke with the cheerful resignation of all women who've learned to live with a man who has sand in his boots. "If you think we should keep going north, Ed, that's what we'll do."

For the Bronson family the journey upstream along the Colorado was very little different from the first leg of the trip that had started in Gila City. The terrain was much the same; the soil was perhaps not quite as loose and sandy, but it was equally arid, and boulders and cacti continued to dominate the landscape. There were still detours to be made around canyons that slashed the land into strips, crawling like long outstretched fingers across the slope that rose from the river, and then still more detours to be made around the bases of mesas that rose abruptly, thrusting their shoulders up without logic or reason. The wagons continued to stop frequently to allow Ed to explore formations that from a distance looked promising, but when reached after a day or half-day of hard walking showed no traces of gold.

At the time the Bronsons' wagons pulled out of Gila City, the short desert winter had been ending. They'd travelled through what was left of the cool season and through the searing cruel days and nights of summer, and before they sighted Fort Mohave a new winter was arriving. The days were cooling and often the thermometer got no higher than eighty or eighty-five degrees, and most of the nights brought gusty winds and swept across the barrens with a chilly bite.

At the fort they stopped long enough to visit the sutler's store and restock their badly depleted supply boxes. Ed couldn't decide whether the sutler was surly by nature or just suffering the aftereffects of a hard night. The man rebuffed all efforts at conversation while their order was being filled, answering Ed's questions with grunts, monosyllables, or simply a nod or shake of his head.

Ed asked, "How far is it to the next town north of here?"

"Vadito? Eight miles."

"Is the road pretty good?" A negative headshake from the sutler. Ed continued, "What kind of town is it?" The answer was a shrug. He persisted, "Well, after we pass Vadito, what's the next settlement to the north?"

"Ain't none."

"Now, there's got to be some kind of towns between here and the border of Canada."

"Mormon settlements. Indian villages."

"What's the country like to the north? Is it much different to the way it is around here?"

"Can't say. Never been north."

At that point only Ed's need for information kept him from giving up. He said, "Down at the Bill Williams River we met a U.S. marshal from up here— Swan's his name. Do you know him?" A nod. "He told me he was after a crazy killer Indian called Gato. Did the marshal ever catch him?"

"Swan stays in Vadito. Ask him."

At Vadito Bronson found Swan getting ready to leave on another trip. When asked about Gato, the marshal said, "No. He always managed to keep a jump or two ahead of me. But if it'll make you feel better, I don't think he's come back this far north. There was a killing a couple of weeks ago down on the Big Sandy. It sounds to me like it was Gato's work. I figure he's still south, maybe in the Buckskin Mountains or the

Harcuvars. I'm heading down there now to see if I can pick up his trail."

"I guess that's good news," Ed said. "I won't be so worried about my womenfolk while I'm out looking."

"Funny thing." Swan's voice was reflective. "Gato's never touched a woman far as anybody knows. If you're planning to stay around here, I'd say you can rest easy."

"That's our plan, to set here a spell. I've heard there's a lot of likely formations on the mesas east of here in the Black Mountain foothills."

"So they say. Not many prospectors are working them right now. Last time I was by Beale Springs there was only two wagons camped there. A year or so ago there'd have been two dozen. The springs is about the best place around here to camp if you're looking for a place to stay a while."

Four wagons were already at Beale Springs when the Bronsons pulled in shortly after sundown. The springs were small, tiny but consistent trickles of water which were caught in natural depressions in the bedrock to form little ponds. In the thin layer of sandy soil bordering the pools a straggle of cottonwoods had rooted and created a miniature oasis.

"I guess the marshal knew what he was talking about," Ed told Amanda as they stood beside the wagons, trying to select a campsite. "This is about as nice a place as we're likely to find. Plenty of clean water, close enough to the mesas and foothills so I can go and come in a day. And it looks like you and Nellie will have some company to visit with."

"We've stayed alone before, Ed. We'll be all right."

"Sure you will. But we've never been in country this wild before. I'll feel better knowing there's people close at hand. And maybe we won't be camping much longer. I've got a real big hunch that my luck's beginning to run strong again."

Amanda was glad, less than a month later, that she hadn't said what she'd been tempted to in reply to Ed's remark about his hunch. For once his luck did run strong. His long days of exploring the mesas, riding Jehosaphat out before daylight and returning long after dark, led to the discovery of a gold vein richer than any strike he'd made before.

"It's not a bonanza," he explained carefully to Amanda after he'd test-worked the vein for several days. "Likely it won't make rich nabobs out of us, and it's going to mean a lot of work to get the gold out. But it's there, Amanda, the lode I've always figured I'd find. I've gone in deep enough so's I know the vein won't peter out in a week or two or even a month or two. It's something I can work for a lot of years. Even if it don't make us rich, it'll give us a good, comfortable life."

Arizona Territory had only two land offices, one in the south at the Presidio of Tucson, the other at the capital in Prescott. Ed left for Prescott the next day to file his claim. When he returned, the Bronsons moved to the claim. They pitched their tent on a long, gently sloping expanse of ground that stretched from the face of the towering cliff where Ed's strike had been made. Ed wasted no time in getting settled. He left that to Amanda and Nellie while he got busy dismantling one of the wagons to get lumber for a flume to run water to the mine from a spring that by an almost unheard of bit of luck he'd broken into while prospecting the face of the cliff above the quartz ledge he'd uncovered.

Bronson discovered very quickly that progress was slow for a lone miner working a quartz vein, much slower than one-man placer mining. He gave himself time, thinking as he worked, then after several months of tunneling into the cliff face, following the thick stratum of quartz in which the gold was embedded, he told Amanda, "I'm losing too much color just running dirt through a sluice the way I'm doing now. I'm going to have to build me an *arrastre*. I figure that'll let me get out about twice as much gold from every shovelful I dig out."

Amanda had spent enough time around gold diggings to know what Ed was talking about. She'd seen *arrastres* at work; primitive versions of a stamping mill that a lone miner could operate with the help of a horse or mule. She knew that Ed planned to build a huge wheel with a wide metal rim that rolled back and forth in a trough or raceway filled with raw ore. When the quartz and rock in the raceway had been pulverized by the wheel, the crushed ore was shoveled into a trough or sluice box with slats nailed in a pattern of repeated *v*'s or *w*'s along its bottom. When water was turned into the sluice, the lighter dirt and stone washed away, leaving the heavy flakes of gold trapped in the slats on the bottom.

"You'll be needing heavy timbers and iron fittings," she reminded him. "Where can you find them around here?"

"I've thought about that. Hadley over in Vadito says the Mormons up at the Beaver Dams settlement have a big blacksmithing works going now. And they've got timber, too, he tells me. That's closer than anyplace but Prescott, and from what I saw there when I went to the land office, a stranger coming in looking for mine fittings cools his heels a long time because the locals always get first call on the blacksmith's time."

"Ed." Amanda's voice was flat, but her eyes were pleading. "Ed, if you're going to get sawed timbers and blacksmith-made fittings, can you get enough lumber and nails to build us a house?"

"Why—" It was an idea that hadn't occurred to him. "I guess so, Manda." He smiled abashedly. "I ought've realized you're getting downright tired of living out of a wagon or in a tent."

"If we're going to stay here, really settle down, don't you think it'd be nice to live like white folks again?"

"Sure it would. You've been real patient with me." He turned to Nellie and said, "You're getting to be a big girl, too. Your old papa's got to remember that one of these days you'll be turning into a young lady who'll need a place to entertain her beaus."

"Oh, that's a long time off, Papa," Nellie replied. "But I guess it would be real nice if we had a regular house like we did out in California."

"All right. Manda, I promise you and Nellie that you'll be sleeping under a roof with wood walls around you before another winter rolls around." Realizing suddenly that he'd let his enthusiasm carry him away, Bronson stopped short and added, "If—"

"If what?" asked Amanda.

"If I can find somebody to lend me a hand. You know how hard it is here to find any men who want to hire out."

"I'll help with the work, Ed, like I always have. And Nellie's strong enough now to help, too."

He shook his head. "No, Manda. This is heavy work I'm getting into. It'll take a strong man to help me lift the timbers that'll go into the *arrastre*. I'll have to look around in Vadito to see if I can find somebody."

Once he'd committed himself to act, Ed Bronson was not a man to waste time. He went to Vadito the next day and came back with a down-on-his-luck prospector who'd been glad enough to earn a grubstake by taking the job Ed offered him. On the following day the two men set out, the prospector driving the stripped-down bed of the wagon that had furnished lumber for the sluice, Ed driving the intact wagon. To reach their destination they had to cross the Colorado at Vadito and follow the stream north; there was no way of getting across the deep canyon through which the river ran on both sides of the Mormon settlement called Beaver Dams.

When they reached the settlement, a sour, strait-laced town with an atmosphere of unfriendly suspicion toward those whom the residents called gentiles, they waited four days while the blacksmith forged and shaped the massive axle and formed from heavy sheet iron the rim of the *arrastre's* wheel and the trough in which it would run. Ed made good use of the time by dickering with the Mormon traders for the heavy timbers he'd need for the wheel and lumber with which to build the house he'd promised Amanda. For the prospector time dragged slowly in a town where he could buy neither tobacco nor liquor nor coffee and where companionship was limited to that of his employer with whom he'd already spent seven boring days on the road.

Ed grated on the man's nerves and he grated on Ed's. Before they left the joyless, suspicious settlement, they were growling at each other. With the wagons so heavily loaded the return trip took nine days instead of the seven they'd spent on the northward journey. Halfway through the trip home their growls turned to snarls, and by the time they reached Vadito, they'd both passed the snarling stage and were not speaking. When they pulled off the ferry, up the rise to town, and stopped in front of the saloon, the prospector broke his silence long enough to demand his pay. When he got it, he invited Ed to take his wagons and his job to hell and quit on the spot.

Stranded twenty miles from the claim with two wagons, one of them without a driver, both of them loaded with materials for a construction project that Ed knew was going to be hard enough for two men to handle and impossible for one, he stood on the steps of the saloon in angry frustration. Before hiring the now defected prospector Ed had searched Vadito for an able-bodied man wanting work and had found none. He was sure the situation hadn't improved during the twenty days he'd been gone.

While he stood there fuming, trying to decide what to do, a man came from between two houses a short distance up the street and began walking toward the saloon. Ed watched him with more interest than he'd usually have shown. At first glance the man looked ageless, then Ed realized that he was young, either a young Mexican or Indian; neither his features nor his clothing gave a firm clue as to which race he belonged. He had the obsidian eyes and wide, square-jawed face and high cheekbones that could have belonged to either race; he wore a headband to secure shoulder-length hair and a tattered denim shirt above equally tattered jeans.

None of this mattered to Bronson. When the man came closer, Ed called, "Hold on a minute. You want a job?" The man turned his head but did not stop or speak. "You," Ed repeated, "I'm talking to you. If you're interested in working, I've got a job open."

Now the man stopped. He stared at Ed for a moment, his face without expression. Finally he asked, "You want me to work for you?"

"That's right." Bronson had never seen the man be-

fore, but he looked husky enough, and this wasn't the
first time he'd stopped a stranger to offer him a job.

"What you want me to do?"

"I'm working a gold mine east of here. I need a man
to help me around the place."

"You pay me?"

"Sure I'll pay you." Ed thought a moment; the going
wage for Mexican and Indian labor was between one
and two dollars a week. He decided to start at the top.
"Two dollars a week and your food."

"How I know you pay me?"

"Hell, if you're worried about that, I'll pay you in
advance." Digging into a pocket of his jeans, Bronson
produced a pair of silver dollars and held them out.
"Here. A week's pay. Take it."

For a moment Ed thought the man was going to re-
fuse, then he stepped forward and took the coins. He
weighed them in his hand, looking first at Ed, then
back in the direction from which he'd come. After a
few seconds of indecision he said, "You wait." He
turned away and hurried back up the street, leaving
Bronson standing there wondering whether he'd hired a
helper or just donated two dollars to a stranger.

Ten minutes passed, then five more; Ed began to get
impatient. He'd just about decided the man wasn't
coming back when he reappeared, running. He stopped
in front of Ed and said, "I work now. What you want
me to do?"

Bronson led him to the wagons. He asked, "You
know how to handle a pair of mules?"

"Mules?" A hearty affirmative nod. "Yes. I know
mules."

A few questions left Ed only half-convinced that his
new helper was telling the truth, but a short ride with
the man handling the reins showed that he could

indeed do a fair job of guiding the team. Ed decided
that the advantage of getting both wagons to the claim
outweighed the slight risk. Within a few minutes the
two teams were moving, Ed leading the way, keeping a
close eye on his new employee in the second wagon.
Slowly the teams dragged the heavily loaded wagons
into the long upslope on their way to the claim.

Chapter
14

"Looks like I lucked out this time," Ed told Amanda. She and Nellie were standing beside him, watching the newly hired helper unload the lumber that was to be used for the new house. The heavier timbers and fittings for the *arrastre* had already been taken off the wagons and stacked near the mine opening. Ed went on, "He's a real willing worker."

"Yes," Amanda agreed. "What's his name?"

"Danged if I know," Ed grinned sheepishly. "I was so tickled to hire him after that fool desert rat quit and left me high and dry that I never got around to asking. And he sure won't take any medals for talking. Didn't say three words all the way out here when we stopped to breathe the mules." Ed raised his voice and called to the man, "Hey, what's your name?"

Deliberately the helper placed the boards he was handling on the neat stack he'd begun behind the tent, then straightened up and faced the Bronsons. He said, "I am Pablo."

"Pablo what?" Amanda asked.

"Pablo," the man replied.

"You're Indian, then," Ed said. "If you was Mexican, you'd have three or four more names to go with Pablo."

Spanish names outnumbered Anglo-Saxon in Arizona Territory after the land's three centuries of Spanish-Mexican rule. Like their predecessors, however, the Anglo newcomers seldom took the trouble to learn the abrupt, multiconsonant languages spoken by the Indians of the territory's many tribes. Spanish remained a lingua franca between Indian and white even after the U.S. took over. Almost all the Indians of any tribe in contact with the whites had two names: their own tribal name, and a Spanish name that had been bestowed on them by a priest or employer or that they had adopted themselves.

When Pablo did not seem inclined to discuss his ancestry, Ed asked him, "What tribe you from, Pablo? Pima? Papago?"

"Not those. I am of the River People."

This could have meant any of several tribes which fitted into the broad "River People" category. Ed decided not to press for more details. "Um. Well, you go on and finish unloading those boards. We'll call you when supper's ready, and I guess you can fix up a shakedown in the wagon. Manda's got some blankets and maybe a spare quilt you can use."

During the following weeks Pablo's position in the life of the claim fell into a familiar and well-established pattern without either him or the Bronsons making any self-conscious adjustment to one another. He continued to work well, steadily if silently, and was quick to understand and follow Ed's directions. Their working day began at full daylight and continued until an hour or so before noon when the blazing heat of the sun directly overhead made outdoor labor almost unbearable. Then after a long siesta break work was resumed and continued until dark.

Actually, Pablo's situation was little different from that of his employers. He slept in the bed of the can-

vas-topped wagon, they slept in the tent. He shared the
food that Amanda cooked at the open hearth of flat
stones Ed had built when they first moved to the claim,
but instead of sitting down with the family, Pablo took
his meals to the wagon and ate them there. He was an
attachment to the Bronson family, not part of it. One
of the contradictions of the American West was that
while it closed the gap between master and servant,
employer and employee, when both were white, the invisible, uncrossable line stood as high as it did in an
Eastern or European mansion when the employer was
white, the employee Mexican or Indian.

At work on the *arrastre* Ed labored as hard as Pablo, both men straining to raise and set the heavy timbers of which its framework was built. A spectator
would have noticed, though, that after starting Pablo to
digging the deep holes in which the cornerposts would
be set, Ed took up the job of measuring and marking
the timbers. Or, after showing Pablo the size and kind
of stones he wanted for the foundation of the ore
trench, Ed would go to work with adze and shave,
shaping the arcs that would form the crusher-wheel
while Pablo levered the rocks out of the stubborn earth
and dragged them into place.

As the *arrastre* took shape, Nellie became a regular
spectator at the spot where it was being built some
thirty yards from the mine opening. After she had
finished helping Amanda wash the breakfast dishes and
get the noonday meal started, there were no set chores
for Nellie to do. On most days she took her place on a
flat rock, her doll across her lap, and watched her father and Pablo at work. After a week or so the men
became so accustomed to seeing the girl's silent figure,
always in the same place, that they paid little attention
to the quiet spectator.

After five weeks of backbreaking work by Ed and Pablo the afternoon arrived when the *arrastre* was finished except for the final job of setting the crusher-wheel in place. The framework was complete—four massive timbers set vertically into the ground formed posts higher than a man's head at the corners of a rectangle twenty feet long and five wide. The posts enclosed a stone foundation on which rested the ore trough. They were braced on three sides to keep them from shifting under the weight of the rolling wheel and were connected by thick stringers that spanned the sides of the rectangle, leaving the ends open. The stringers were anchored firmly to the tops of the uprights; they formed a parallel track that would carry the great wheel's metal hub-flanges as it rolled back and forth in the runway made by the trough. Stop-blocks had already been spiked to one end of each stringer, and blocks for the still unenclosed end lay ready to be fastened down after the wheel was placed. These blocks limited the wheel's travel to the length of the heavy sheet metal ore trough.

A few yards from the open end of the frame the crusher-wheel lay on its side, balanced on one of the flanges that extended beyond the hub and were actually part of that sturdy metal forging. When the wheel was in place, the flanges would roll along the parallel stretcher beams. From the wheel's hub radiated spokes bigger than a man's thigh, and to their outer ends were bolted crescent-shaped arcs hewn from thick boards. Joined together on the wheel, the arcs formed a circle over which was fitted the wide sheet iron rim that would pulverize the ore when the wheel rolled along in the trough. As it rested waiting to be hoisted into place, the wheel was an impressive sight, ten feet in diameter, almost three feet thick, and weighing well over a ton.

Assembling the wheel and bolting on its metal rim had required almost a full day, and when the rim was secured in place, Ed looked at the sun beginning to slant far to the west. "If we get right on it," he told Pablo, "we can lift that thing in place today. I'd sure like to see it, too, because I haven't sluiced a shovelful of dirt for too long now."

Anticipating the wheel's completion, they'd already erected the gear Ed had designed to use in hoisting the big wheel into position after he'd seen that assembling the wheel inside the *arrastre*'s framework wasn't possible. For the tripod Ed had used three of the foot-square timbers twenty feet long that he'd bought for the foundation of the house that still had to be built. The timbers, placed as closely as possible to the end of the *arrastre*'s frame, rose high over the cornerposts. Their base ends had been sunk into the earth and braced with stakes, their tops lashed and spiked together. From the tripod's peak a block and tackle dangled.

"Nellie," Ed said, "You run down to the tent and tell your mama while I bring up the mules from the corral. Tell her we're just about to finish up this job if she'll lend us a hand."

Within a few minutes preparations for the hoisting were completed. Ed, Amanda, and Pablo stood close to the wheel; Nellie had returned to her usual place on the rock nearby.

"Now, here's what we'll do," Ed said. "We hitch all four mules to the wheel and skid it under the tripod. Manda, you handle the mules while Pablo and me keep the wheel level and lever it out if it hangs up on a rock or digs into the ground. Just keep the mules moving, Manda, straight and slow."

Amanda nodded. "All right, Ed. I've handled the mules enough to keep them moving straight."

Bronson continued, "Once the wheel's under the tackle, we'll hitch three mules to the block. Manda, you work them. I'll put Jehoshaphat to the wheel, and once it clears the ground, I'll lead him straight from the end of the frame while Pablo steadies the wheel and sorta guides it between the stringers. You got that, Pablo?"

"Yes. I understand."

Dragging the wheel into place under the tripod went smoothly, though Ed and Pablo had to use all their strength to keep the huge rim from dipping down and the bottom hub gouged a deep trench in the stone-hard soil. A rope had already been reeved through the tackle blocks, and Ed quickly lashed it to the wheel's rim while Pablo helped Amanda change the mules' harness. When Ed came over for Jehoshaphat's rein, Amanda was looking frowningly at the rope that descended from the blocks.

"Ed, are you sure that rope's stout enough? This wheel must weigh a ton or more."

"Well, it better be stout enough, honey, because it's the best rope we got. Come right down to it, it's the only rope we got that's long enough to do the job. Now, don't worry, Manda. This is the same tackle we've used a dozen times to raise and lower the wagons over cliffs. We'll be all right if everybody remembers to move smooth and easy."

With the three mules straining in their collars, the wheel tilted grudgingly until it stood upright, its wide rim resting on the ground. The hub with its protruding flanges was more than a foot below the level of the stringers on which it would roll.

Ed called, "Hold the mules right there, Manda, let 'em breathe a minute before they take on the big load." To Pablo he said, "Now, when that wheel comes off the ground, it's going to want to spin. Be sure you aim it straight into the frame and hold it straight while I pull it into place."

Pablo nodded. Bronson studied the rope, taut now between the blocks. "Seems to be holding all right. Let's lift it."

He led Jehoshaphat between the stringers to the far end of the framework until the rope between mule and heel was taut. Then he called, "All right, Manda! Go ahead!"

Amanda geed the mules she was leading. The pulleys creaked in protest and the tripod's foot-square timbers sank deeper into the ground as they took the full weight of the massive wheel. Slowly, though, it rose. Standing behind it, Pablo wrapped his arms around the rim, holding it in line with the opening between the *arrastre's* parallel frames. Amanda's mules leaned harder into their harness in response to her steady pull on their reins. Inch by inch the wheel rose from the ground until the hub-flanges were just above the level of the stringers. Ed, watching closely, started Jehoshaphat forward. Like a huge pendulum, the wheel began to swing toward the frame.

To bring the hub-flange over the ends of the stringers, it was necessary to move the wheel almost six feet from the spot directly under the tripod's apex where it first cleared the ground. Ed had instructed Amanda to back the three mules she was handling very slowly to compensate for the wheel's forward motion. She saw him leading Jehoshaphat ahead, but when she slackened her reins to start the three mules backing, they balked and kept straining forward. Ed, concentrating on his own part of the task, kept Jehoshaphat steadily tugging the wheel forward.

Stress has its own way of finding weak spots, in both inanimate objects and in men. The rope that held the wheel suspended began to sing. The song quickly changed into an angry whine. A small spot in one of the strands—perhaps where a half dozen of its manila fibers had frayed on a rock at some time in the past while the wagon was being lowered into a canyon—began to fuzz up. As the strain increased, the frizzed spot began to grow wider, more fibers breaking down, until the weakened strand broke and began unravelling in both directions from the break. The two remaining strands could not hold the heavy load. They snapped simultaneously with a crack as loud as a rifleshot. The huge wheel, barely over the stringers, plunged downward.

Amanda's mules lurched forward when their load slackened, and she found herself tangled in a maze of loose curling reins. Ed could not bring Jehoshaphat to a quick halt; the animal kept pulling—fortunately, for it gave the wheel enough forward momentum to bring the hub-flanges well over the stringer. Pablo lost his grip on the wheel and lunged ahead, stumbling. Before he could get hold of the wheel again the pulley released. The broken rope came sailing down from the tripod toward him. The rope, trailing from the flying pulley, entangled Pablo like a half-dozen lariats dropped over him at the same time. He lost his footing just as the pulley struck him a glancing, stunning blow on the head. Pablo fell across the ore trough.

With an echoing thud the hubs hit the stringers. For a moment or so the wheel bounced straight up and down. Ed had by this time managed to halt his mule, but the wheel gained its own momentum. It stopped bouncing, rolled along the stringers, hit the stop-blocks at their ends, halted quivering for a space of seconds, then reversed its direction and began rolling back toward the spot where Pablo lay, his sprawled body spanning the sharp edges of the metal trough.

Nellie was closer to the *arrastre* than either Ed or Amanda. She reacted, more from the memory of having chocked wagon wheels at canyon rims than from any planned intent. The stop-blocks that were to be placed at the end of the stringers after the wheel had been positioned were laying at the foot of the upright nearest her. Nellie jumped up, letting her doll fall unnoticed to the ground, and ran to the *arrastre*. Picking up one of the bulky stop-blocks, she dropped it into the ore trough between the dazed man and the moving crusher-wheel.

In its few feet of travel since rebounding from the end of the frame the wheel had not picked up enough speed to jump the barrier Nellie put in its path. The wide iron rim crunched into the chunk of wood, pushed it a few inches along the bottom of the trough, and the wheel shuddered to a stop.

Ed by now had halted Jehoshaphat, and Amanda had shaken free of the entangling reins. Both ran to the *arrastre*, and after assuring themselves that Nellie was unhurt they looked to Pablo. Ed kneeled by the trough and began untangling the loops of rope coiled around the young Indian. Pablo stirred, his eyes opened, he tried to sit up.

"Better just lay quiet," Ed advised him. "You took a pretty good whack from that block. Manda's gone to the tent for the whiskey bottle, and after you've had a drink to perk you up, we'll see how bad you're hurt."

"I am not hurt." Pablo pushed himself into a sitting position. The movement brought a grimace of pain flickering over his face. He felt his head gingerly and repeated, "I am not hurt."

"You don't look very chipper, though," Amanda said, arriving with a cup of steaming liquid. "Here, drink this. I had the kettle on, so I just made you a hot toddy. It'll do you more good than straight whiskey."

Pablo drank the toddy, though his lips twisted with dislike as he brought the cup away from his mouth. "It tastes like swampgrass root drink Paiute women brew. Anything that tastes so bad must be good medicine."

Ed said, "I'm going to hitch up the wagon real quick. It'll be dark before we get to Fort Mohave, but I'm going to take you there and have the Army doctor look you over."

"No! I want no *hyko* doctor!" Pablo struggled to his feet and managed to stand without too much wavering with Ed's hand steadying him. He said, "Let us go on with the work."

Ed indicated the wheel, resting now atop the stringers. "The work's finished. At least for right now."

"You'd be finished, too, except for Nellie," Amanda told Pablo. "If she hadn't run and put that block under the wheel, it'd've cut you into pieces."

Moving slowly, still unsteady on his feet, Pablo turned to look at the *arrastre*. A glance was enough to tell him what had happened. He stared gravely at Nellie for a few moments, then said, "This is a good thing you have done. I, Pablo, will not forget it."

Chapter
15

"Will you stop worrying about Pablo, Ed?" Amanda put a plate of bacon and hotcakes on the table in front of her husband. "This is only the fourth day he's been gone."

Ed didn't reply at once. He attacked his breakfast angrily, oblivious to the rosy sunrise that painted the cool night-washed desert sky. When he'd eaten a few bites, he said, "Pablo told me he'd just be away a couple of days. If he'd said four days, I might not've been so willing for him to take time off. Work's stacking up."

"You know how Indians are about time," she reminded him. Then she added thoughtfully, "He might've been hurt worse than we thought he was. You know how we heard him carrying on, that night the pulley hit him. Groaning and whimpering like he couldn't stop. Maybe you should've taken him to the doctor, whether he wanted to go or not."

Ed shook his head. "He acted like he was afraid of white men's doctors. Anyhow, I looked at the place, all he got was a pretty good bump. If it'd been a cut or something like that, I'd've insisted, but I didn't feel it was up to me to force him."

"I suppose. Well, the chances are he'll be back to-day."

Although Nellie was now in her teens, she was still bashful about interrupting conversations between her parents. She waited until it was obvious neither Ed nor Amanda was going to say anything more, then volunteered, "I can help you, Papa, if Pablo doesn't come back."

"Now, that's real sweet of you," Ed smiled. He reached across the rough, narrow table and patted her cheek. "I guess if it came down to a real tight, you'd make me a pretty good hand. But I can manage by myself for a while." He turned to Amanda. "I tried running an *arrastre* single-handed yesterday, and it wasn't too bad. Crushed up some old tailings from the sluice box and ran the crushing through again. Got out more color than I did when I put the ore through the old sluice box the first time."

"Why, that's fine, Ed. But you'll still need help, won't you?"

"Sure. With another man working, I can take out twice as much ore and handle it twice as fast. Even by myself, though, I'll get out as much color in a day as I did with just the sluice. And you know what that means, Manda?"

"I hope it's what I think it does."

"Yep. It means I can start building your new house."

"Not if it's going to crowd you. We've stood the tent this long, it won't hurt us to stay in it a little bit longer."

"I guess we can stand most anything we can't cure, but I want to get that house built and us settled into it before another winter rolls around." He grinned at Nellie. "And don't you worry, young lady. There'll be plenty of work for everybody once we get started."

"Then you're going to start building by yourself, even if Pablo doesn't come back?"

"You just bet I am. I promised you and Nellie a house, and a house is what you're going to have. But I expect you're right about Pablo, Manda. He'll probably show up today."

Amanda's prophecy proved correct. Pablo returned shortly before noon, obviously weary, but fit enough to pitch in and do his share of the work. Ed asked how he felt and how his trip had been; so did Amanda when she dished up his supper. To both of them, and to both questions, Pablo responded with only one word, "Good."

Pablo had never been talkative, but it seemed to Ed that he was even more silent than usual as they worked side by side the following day. They put the final touches on the *arrastre*, smoothing a track from the mine entrance to the ore trough along which a mule could drag a rock sled loaded with ore. That done, they set a post and the rope tackle for the trip-windlass around which the same mule would walk and roll the big crusher-wheel back and forth. Their last task was to dismantle the temporary hoist and haul the big timbers down to the site Amanda had selected for the new house. It was almost dark when the timbers were moved and stacked, and only then did Pablo break his almost total day-long silence.

"Do you want me to go now?" he asked Ed.

"Go? Go where? Damn it, Pablo, you just got back."

"But I did not come back when I promised I would. And the big machine is finished—there is no more work to do on it."

Happy with the day's progress, Ed had sloughed off his anger of the morning hours. He grinned at Pablo. "Is that what's been biting at you all day? Thought I was going to run you off just because you showed up a little bit late?"

"But the work is finished—" Pablo began.

Ed interrupted him. "Work's never finished around a place like this one, Pablo. And about you being late, forget it."

"But, I thought—"

"Whatever you thought, it was wrong. You're a pretty good worker and you got a job here as long as you want it. Now, I got a hunch Amanda's about got supper ready. Come on, let's go eat."

Most of the big flat stones close to the mine had been used in building the *arrastre*. The following morning Ed sent Pablo with the wagon to begin hauling suitable stones for the foundation on which the new house would rest. While he waited for the first load of stones, Ed kept busy, pegging out the foundation lines and marking timbers to be cut as soon as Pablo returned to pull one end of the bucksaw. He was marking the end of a timber for squaring when Hank Swan rode up on his buckskin.

"Morning, Bronson," Swan called. He swung out of the saddle and dropped the reins over the horse's head.

"Marshal," Bronson nodded. He straightened up and walked over to Swan. The two men shook hands. Ed said, "You're out early."

"Don't know whether you'd say it's early or late. I been out most of the night."

"I guess you could use some coffee, then. I'll call Amanda."

"Wait just a minute before you do. I want to talk private."

"What's the trouble?" Bronson frowned.

"Well." Swan pushed his broad-brimmed hat to the

back of his head. "I don't want to get you folks all upset, but it looks like Gato's come back."

"Lord-a-mighty, Marshal! I thought he'd left this
part of the country for good. There hasn't been one of
those mysterious killings around here for—how long?
A year or two, anyhow."

"Right at two years. I figured about the same way
you did, that he'd left the territory or maybe got killed
himself."

"Who'd he kill now? Another soldier at the fort?"

"It was a soldier," Swan nodded. "But not at the
fort. This one was a despatch rider. He was killed on
the way from the fort to that new outpost they set up
down at Warm Springs."

"When did it happen?"

"Can't say exactly. I haven't found out yet whether
the man was going or coming back. He's been gone
from the fort for more than a week."

"You're sure it was Gato?"

"As sure as makes no never-mind. Throat cut ear to
ear, but not scalped like he'd've been if the Mohaves
had got him. Body wasn't robbed, either, except for his
rifle and ammunition. I talked to the Pima tracker the
captain sent down before I ever got word there was a
killing, and the tracker said he'd found signs that
showed it was Gato's style."

"How could he be sure?" Bronson frowned. "Unless
the tracker'd been after Gato before?"

"He had. Said Gato played dead just off the trail,
and when the rider stopped and dismounted and went
to look, Gato just reached up and slashed his head almost off."

"And did he find signs Gato headed this way afterward?"

Swan shook his head. "Can't say for sure. The Pima

lost the tracks about a hundred yards from where the killing happened. He's going back with me and swing some circles to see if he can pick up a trail after Gato quit hiding his tracks."

"Just the same, you're pretty well sure that's who done it?"

"I'm mortal certain, Ed. That's why I stopped by, to warn you, just like I'm warning everybody else that's located out from town the way you are. And to ask if you've seen any stray Indians hanging around lately."

"Not a one, Marshal. Except Pablo. But you couldn't rightly call him a stray. He's been working for me more than four months now."

"Works steady, does he?"

"Every day." Bronson pointed to the *arrastre*. "We just finished that up a few days ago, and I give him some time off. But he got back all right. He's out with the wagon now. I'm getting ready to put up a real board house for the family, and I sent him out to get some foundation stones. He'll be back pretty soon if you want to talk to him. He might've noticed something I didn't while he was off."

"Tell me what he looks like."

"Well, hell, Marshal, you know all the Indians in this part of the country look pretty much the same. Let's see. Pablo's not real old—I'd guess maybe twenty-five, but it's hard to tell their age. He's about the same shade of brown as the rest of 'em, got black hair and black eyes." Bronson's brow furrowed. "You told me one time that nobody'd ever seen Gato. Does that still hold?"

"Yes. I don't know any more about him now than I did when I started looking for him. That scar he's supposed to have on his arm is still all I've got to go by. I don't guess your man Pablo's got a scarred arm, has he? You've been working alongside of him, you'd notice a thing like that."

"If he's got any scars, I don't recall seeing 'em. And like you say, working with him every day, I'd've noticed if he had any."

Swan said with finality, "I don't see an Indian like Gato as being the kind who'd hang around any sort of job for very long, knowing everybody was looking for him."

"Well, Pablo don't strike me as being a killer," Bronson volunteered. "He's about as quiet and peaceful as you'd want."

"Sure. But just the same, you and your womenfolk be real careful. Keep a close lookout for strangers."

"Don't worry, we will," Bronson promised. "Amanda's not scared of anything, any more than I am. And we both watch Nellie pretty close."

"Might be a good idea if you wear a gunbelt while you're at work," Swan suggested. "And if you go out ᵣ place, especially by yourself, remember to look back over your shoulder now and then."

"I'll do that, Marshal."

"If anything else happens, I'll ride out or send somebody to tell you the news. The main thing is, be careful."

"We will be. Now, let's go see if we can't scare up some coffee. You look like you could use a cup."

For several weeks after Swan's visit Ed Bronson followed the marshal's advice. He wore his gunbelt wherever he went, even though it got in his way at times as he and Pablo worked on the new house. He kept a closer watch than usual, but saw no lurking strangers—saw nothing unusual; just the same scurrying lizards, once or twice a snake winding sinuously away, an occasional soaring hawk, on one occasion a kit fox pattering off in the dawn. Swan did not return or send anyone with fresh news, and as the days slipped past, the feeling of imminent danger the marshal's visit had brought faded and was forgotten.

Day followed busy day without incident. The new house rose with surprising speed on its foundation of flat stones and heavy timbers. Wide pine boards set vertically on the studding formed its walls, the cracks between the boards closed with narrow battens. The roof was framed, then covered with rippled sheets of corrugated iron nailed to the low-pitched rafters.

"You can't rightly call it a palace," Ed told Amanda and Nellie as they stood a little distance from the house, looking at its walls of yet unpainted yellow pine glowing in the low sun of late afternoon. "But it's a sight better than a tent."

"I think it's beautiful, Papa," Nellie said. "I like it better than any of the houses I remember us living in when I was just a little girl."

"Nellie's right, Ed," Amanda agreed. "It's a fine house, and I'm going to enjoy it more for having waited for it such a long time. How soon can we move in?"

"Just as soon as I can get the trim work done, and I figure that'll take me about a week after I get back from Prescott."

"Prescott?" There was surprise in Amanda's voice. "The way Vadito's grown up, I thought you'd get the rest of what you need from there."

"I wish I could, Manda, but there's five bidders for every board and nail that's hauled into Vadito these days. Last time I bought nails there I paid three dollars a pound. Besides, I need things I can't get in Vadito, window sash and glass panes, some good straight-grained pine boards for the inside walls, paint and doorhinges, a pretty good list of stuff. Quickest way to get it is to go to Prescott, buy it on the spot, and haul it back."

"Ed?" Amanda's tone was tentative. "Will you have room on the wagon for some furniture, too?"

"Some. What've you got in mind?"

"A stove's the main thing. You don't know how much I've missed a good kitchen range. A double bed for us and a half-bed for Nellie. Some chairs and a table, if there's room."

"You make up a list," Ed told her. "I'll bring back all I can." He turned to Nellie. "How about you, honey? You want anything from Prescott?"

"Well—" She hesitated, then held up her doll. "Do you think we could get a bed for Rosie, too?"

Ed chucked her chin. "I'll sure try. And if I can't find one that fits her, I'll make you one the first extra time I've got after I get back."

Amanda asked, "How long will you be gone?"

"Let's see. Takes four days each way riding Jehoshaphat, so allow an extra day going in the wagon, two days extra coming back with a full load. A day in town, maybe two."

"Will you take Pablo with you to help?"

Ed shook his head. "Not unless you're afraid to have him on the claim without me being around."

"Afraid of Pablo? Of course not! I just thought you'd want him to help you because there's nothing much he can do here while you're away."

"There is, though. I'm going to set him digging out a place on the face of the cliff, up above the mine where the spring comes out, where I can put a water tank. There's a cooper's shop in Prescott where I can get the staves and hoops. If I put a tank up there by that spring, it'll give a good steady flow for the sluice box, and then later I can run a little flume or maybe even find pipe enough to reach down to the house. It'll save building a cistern for you."

"My goodness!" Amanda smiled. "It'll be almost like living in town when you get everything finished. I won't know how to act, a house with real board floors and glass windows, a kitchen stove, and water right to my door!"

Ed's voice was sober. "Manda, I know you'd've rather we went to a town somewheres when we left Gila City. You've been real good putting up with everything. So I'm going to do whatever I can to make living out here as easy as possible. Might as well, because it looks to me like we've found a place where we're going to be living for a long, long time."

Chapter
16

Although both Amanda and Nellie were very much aware of Ed Bronson's absence after he'd left for Prescott, there was little change in the tempo of the days on the claim. There were still three meals a day to be prepared, dishes and pots to be washed, bedding to be aired, rips in clothing to be mended, buttons sewed on. These were among the jobs that mother and daughter had begun sharing soon after Nellie's twelfth birthday.

With Ed away Amanda's work was lessened to a degree. There were no dirt-crusted, sweat-caked jeans and shirts to be scrubbed daily on a washboard, using shavings of hard brown soap that stubbornly resisted dissolving or forming lather in the hard water. Wood was too scarce to be used recklessly, so Amanda did not heat the laundry boiler more often than once a week. Ed's work clothes were washed in cold water, rinsed repeatedly, and hung over the tent's guy-ropes to dry.

Amanda found herself with leisure moments for the first time since they'd been living on the claim. She spent most of them sitting in the bare, almost finished house, planning the places where she'd have Ed build the partitions that would make a big main room, a bedroom for them, and a smaller bedroom for Nellie. After she'd decided how the interior was to be partitioned, she went on to visualize the way she'd arrange the furniture. She picked out the exact spot where her new kitchen range would sit, the best location for the table, the handiest and coolest spots to locate the beds. Then she began deciding on the colors and rufflings of the curtains she'd put at the windows as soon as the windows were finished and she could get Ed to take her into Vadito to buy material.

Nellie's day changed less than did her mother's. The routine of their shared chores was unaltered, but Nellie was still too young to share Amanda's pleasure in projecting the bare interior of the house into furnished, liveable rooms. While Amanda was daydreaming inside, Nellie continued the habit of work-watching she'd gotten into while her father and Pablo were building the *arrastre*.

Following the instructions Ed had given him before leaving, Pablo was cutting the shelf on the cliff face above the mine to make a place for the new water tank. Each morning when her household jobs had been done, Nellie cradled Rosie in one arm and walked up from the tent to the cliff. She settled on the rock where she'd been accustomed to sitting while Ed and Pablo were digging the mine opening and later when they'd been working on the *arrastre*. Pablo was now working higher up on the cliff face, though, and after a few mornings of watching him swing pick and shovel Nellie grew tired of holding her head at such an uncomfortable upward tilt. One morning instead of stopping at the rock, Nellie climbed up the sketchy ledge Pablo had dug out to the location of the tank and found a place to sit closer to where he was working.

Seeing her appear at the edge of the shelf, Pablo stopped work. He stood watching, a shovelful of dirt poised ready to swing, until Nellie sat down. When he saw she planned to stay, he asked, "Does the lady know you would climb up?"

"No. But it's all right. She knows I always come here to watch you and Papa."

Pablo shook his head. "He is not here now. And this place is not like the other on the ground below. If you were to fall and be hurt, I would be blamed."

"Pooh. I'm not a baby. I won't fall off."

Nellie's presence presented Pablo with a situation that puzzled and upset him. He was fully aware of the invisible barrier that stood between him and his employer's family and sensed that neither Ed nor Amanda would approve of Nellie climbing up the cliff. He knew, too, that it was not his place to scold or to give orders and after thinking things over, decided that whatever he did would be wrong, so he did nothing. With a nod that told Nellie he accepted her presence but didn't approve of it, he went back to work.

For a while Nellie watched in silence as Pablo gouged into the hard, stubborn soil with his pick and shoveled the loosened dirt off the shelf. Soon, though, she began to miss some element that had always been part of her watching before. This puzzled her until she'd thought about it for a few moments and concluded that what was missing was the conversation—always sparing and always confined to their job—that broke the silence when Ed and Pablo were working together.

After a few minutes she asked, "What did you do before you came to work for Papa?"

"Many things." Pablo did not look up from his digging.

"Did you work for somebody else?"

"Yes."

"Where?"

"Many places."

"For other white people?"

"Yes."

"Is that how you learned to talk English?"

"Yes."

Irritated by his monosyllabic replies, Nellie snapped, "Why won't you talk to me, Pablo? You and Papa talk to each other."

"That is not the same."

"I don't see why not. I'm here and you're here. You never have anybody but Papa to talk to. I never have anybody but him and Mama to talk to. And Rosie."

"Rosie?" Pablo frowned, puzzled. He'd seen Nellie carrying the doll many times and because of the care with which she handled it, had assumed it must be some kind of special clan symbol or totem. Although he'd wondered about the doll's significance, he'd never asked about it. From childhood Pablo had been taught that to inquire about or even to notice overtly the clan symbol of another was not only impolite, but could bring misfortune to both the totem's owner and the one who asked about it.

Nellie held up the doll. "This is Rosie, silly."

Pablo now concluded that since Nellie had displayed the doll and called his attention to it, no bad luck would follow if he asked about it. He came closer and reached out a hand tentatively to touch the doll, but drew his hand back quickly before his fingers reached Rosie's blond curls. He asked, "Is it forbidden for another than you to touch the Rosie?"

"Of course not." Nellie held the doll out to him. "Here. You can hold her if you'll be careful not to drop her."

Gingerly Pablo took the doll. He felt the hard, cool

surface of its painted bisque face and hands, passed his fingers over the wiry softness of its blond wig.

"You talk to the Rosie?" he asked. He knew the answer, for he'd heard her doing so, but somehow needed her affirmation. Nellie nodded. He asked, "Does she talk to you?"

"Only pretend-talk. She's only a doll."

"Pretend-talk?" There was no equivalent for the phrase in Pablo's vocabulary. "Doll?" This was another new concept to him.

"A toy to play with," she explained. Then, seeing that Pablo did not understand, she asked, "Didn't you have any toys to play with when you were a little boy?"

"Toys?" Pablo was still bewildered. It was the bewilderment of one to whom the concept of a toy except as a small-scale replica of a tool or weapon that would be used throughout life, the concept of play except as training for growing up, was alien to understanding.

Nellie saw that Pablo was struggling to grasp the ideas she'd offered so casually. She repeated, "Toys. Didn't you have any?"

Pablo shook his head. "What are these things?"

"To play with. Like Rosie."

"You have the only Rosie I have ever seen."

Nellie sighed. "I'll explain about toys."

During the next half hour she tried to convey to Pablo the thought of toys and of children playing for their own enjoyment in a leisure that he had never experienced. As she talked, he interrupted now and then with a question. At some point in their interchange his shyness and caution melted, the invisible wall between white master and Indian servant was forgotten.

Nellie's explanations left Pablo somewhat confused, and his questions did little to make clear the ideas she was trying to pass on to him. Pablo could get no real understanding of a civilization in which it had become unnecessary to train children from infancy in nothing except methods of self-defense or attack and methods by which they could survive in a harsh land. Their talk did establish communication between him and Nellie, and that was enough. Before the day ended, they were talking to each other without constraint, and during the following days as Pablo completed his job of clearing the shelf on the cliff face, the hours Nellie spent watching him were no longer silent ones.

With Ed Bronson's return and the resumption of work on the house the talking between Nellie and Pablo ended by unspoken agreement. Neither the girl nor the Indian could have put the reason for this into words, but both knew by instinct that if either of them gave any indication that the wall between them had been breached, the adult Bronsons would have been first dismayed, then alarmed, and finally angered. After Ed returned, he and Pablo still worked side by side, their talk confined to the jobs they were doing. Nellie still watched them, but once more in silence. Only on the rare occasions when Ed left the work area for a few moments did Nellie and Pablo exchange a few hurried words or a nod and a smile.

Completion of the new house came suddenly, almost unexpectedly, as long-anticipated events so often do. As soon as the last boards of the interior walls had been nailed in place, Amanda and Nellie joined the men in a frenzy of painting. Ed and Pablo brushed red barn paint on the exterior while the women worked inside, applying coats of white to the interior walls.

Then there was the moving. Ed pulled away the tarpaulins that had been spread over the new furniture; he and Pablo carried the pieces inside. Under

Amanda's excited supervision the men assembled the beds and placed them as she directed and at last brought in the new kitchen range and put it in the precise spot she'd chosen for it.

Ed Bronson looked around. "Well, you're moved in," he told his wife. "Now me and Pablo can get back to the mine."

"Not until you're through here," she announced. "Don't forget those boxes and crates and those two barrels we've been carrying around with us since we left California. They've got to be brought in and opened up and unpacked first."

"Can't they wait?"

"No, they can't, Ed. They've got things in them that I'll need, now we've got a real house to live in."

"Things like what?"

"Glasses and chinaware. And little personal pretties a woman likes to have in her home."

"Well." Bronson shook his head. "I guess I might as well get at them now as later. I don't expect you'd give me much rest until you've got everything brought inside and put away like you want it."

A half day later he shook his head again at the profusion of "little pretty things a woman likes to have in her home" that were stacked high on every flat surface inside the house.

"I'm going to need more shelves," Amanda said, vigorously sweeping out the shreds of straw and dusty litter that remained after the unpacking of the boxes and barrels that had remained untouched for so many years. "Maybe even a sideboard of some kind next time you go to Prescott. There was a lot more stuff in those boxes than I remembered."

"A lot more'n I did, too," he replied. "All I recall is

how heavy them things got after I'd loaded and un-
loaded the wagons."

"How about my shelves?" she asked.

"They'll just have to wait. I'm out of lumber. I'll
pick some up next time I go to Vadito." Ed surveyed
the array of plates and glassware that overflowed to the
floor and was stacked along one wall of the main room
of the new house. "And I've got to get the mine going
full time again. You'll just have to make do as best you
can for a little while."

Imperceptibly in the months that passed after the
house was finished and occupied, the final touches were
added and new daily routines became established.
Amanda, for so many years without a house to keep in
order, found an endless succession of small tasks to occupy her and Nellie. She smiled to herself as she saw
her daughter beginning to acquire the skills she'd had
no chance to learn during the nomadic years when the
Bronsons were moving from one temporary home to
another, living much of the time in a tent or in the bed
of a wagon.

There was still construction to occupy the men during the first weeks after the house was completed. They
assembled the staves that Ed had bought, precut, and
fitted, from the cooperage shop in Prescott, and drove
the iron hoops tight around them to make the water
tank. From the tank they ran new flumes, a large one
to the sluice box, and from its outlet a second, smaller
flume to a stone-lined cistern that they built behind the
house. Finally, with boards and timbers bought at a ru-
inous price in Vadito, they put up a big toolshack near
the mine entrance, large enough to include space for a
bunk for Pablo.

These were spare-time jobs, done during periods
stolen or borrowed from the operation of the mine.

Once the odd job list had been completed, Ed began to work the mine full time. He and Pablo spent all their daytime hours digging ore out of the steadily deepening shaft, crushing it in the *arrastre*, and washing it through the sluice box to extract the gold. Their routine was broken only by Ed's monthly trips to Vadito, which had burgeoned into a bustling town, where he bought supplies and deposited the month's accumulation of raw gold at the new Wells Fargo office.

"I better figure to go into Vadito a little earlier this month," Ed said to Amanda as they were preparing for bed one night. He'd just added another bag of gold, ranging from tiny, almost invisible flakes to nuggets as big as a man's thumb, to the cache he'd built into the floor under their bed. "Since we've got back to working the mine full time, and with the *arrastre* boosting up the yield, the gold seems to pile up faster than it used to. And I don't like to keep so much of it on hand here. The way the country's getting so filled up with people nowadays, you never know who's apt to come riding up the road, or what they've got in mind."

"We do see more faces now," Amanda agreed. "Why, it used to be months would go by without anybody coming near the place. Now it seems like we get a visitor every week or two." A thought occurred to her. "Maybe that's why I seem to be running out of food faster than I did. If somebody's visiting and it gets to be mealtime, their name goes into the pot, too."

"Sure. It's not like we were pinched, though, Manda. Don't worry about a little extra food. We can afford it."

"That's not what bothers me. It's running short like I've been doing the past two or three months and not knowing why. Well, if you're going to town soon, I'll start making my list, and I'll get a little bit more of everything this time."

Ed was just dropping off to sleep when Amanda wakened him by suddenly sitting upright in the bed. "Ed! It's just dawned on me why I'm running short of supplies. It's not the people visiting us. It's Pablo."

"You mean he's been taking food out of your supply boxes? Why'd he do a thing like that, Manda? We've always fed him good."

"I don't think he's stealing. He's just piling enough food for two on his plate every time he comes for a meal."

"Don't you still dish up for him?"

"No. For a while right after we moved into the house, I always seemed to have my hands full doing something else when he'd come down for his meal, so I started letting him just help himself."

"I don't see anything wrong with that. He works hard, we can't grudge him what all he eats."

"I'm not begrudging him. I just remembered that about the middle of last month he began heaping up his plate. Like I said a minute ago, he takes enough for two now."

"Maybe his appetite's just got bigger."

"Not all that much bigger, not just all of a sudden. And he's certainly not putting on any more weight." A ghost of worry crept into Amanda's voice. "Ed, could he maybe be feeding somebody else? Some Indian friend of his who's in trouble?"

"Not hardly likely, Manda. If there was anybody hanging around the claim, I'd've been sure to see 'em."

"Maybe not. Now that I think about it, he doesn't always take more food than usual." She frowned, trying to remember. "Always at supper, but not always at noon. When you're not going right back up to the mine, he takes an extra big helping, but if you're going up there right away, he doesn't."

"And after supper I generally stay down here at the house," Ed mused. "Well, if you put it that way, I guess it could be possible. It sure won't take me long to find out, Manda. I'll just have a look-see tomorrow night after supper."

When Amanda rang the big dinner bell the next evening to signal Pablo to bring his plate for supper, Bronson waited until he saw his Indian helper coming toward the house. As Pablo entered by the kitchen door, Ed slipped out the front door and hurried up the path to the mouth of the mine. He stopped long enough to take a quick look in the toolshed; it was empty as he'd been sure it would be. Then he moved into the yawning mouth of the mine only a few yards away.

Peering out cautiously, he watched Pablo return, balancing a plate heaped high with food. Pablo went into the shed. Ed waited, glancing out of the tunnel now and then, listening carefully for noises of any approaching footsteps. Twilight faded and the sky shaded slowly from a deep translucent blue in the east to a narrowing strip of baby-pink on the western horizon.

Ed had just about decided that Amanda's hunch had been wrong when he heard the toolshed door creak. He took a cautious look from the concealment of the mine entrance and saw the Indian walking away from the shed, still carrying the plate. The heaps of food on it had not been touched. Giving him a few steps start, Ed followed Pablo around the cliff. Pablo walked fast, following the ledge down to the base of the towering butte and keeping close to it. He came to a spot where a small, jagged slit slashed the hillside, the opening of a little box canyon. Pablo vanished into the slit.

After waiting a few moments Ed moved up and looked into the opening. A few yards inside the canyon's mouth Pablo had seated himself on a smaller boulder. Beside him there sat another figure, eating. In the dim, fast-fading light it took several seconds for Ed to realize that Pablo's companion was a woman.

Stepping into the canyon mouth, Ed said in a quiet voice, "You want to tell me about your lady friend, Pablo?"

Before Ed had finished speaking, Pablo was on his feet and had turned to face his employer. Darkness veiled his features, but when he spoke, Ed got the impression that his voice was being held in careful control.

Pablo said, "She is more than a friend. This is my mother."

"Your mother!" Bronson exclaimed.

Behind Pablo the woman stood up. Straining to see her, Ed could make out only the shadow of a sad, scarred face and a pair of glistening black eyes. She looked steadily at him, saying nothing.

Incredulously Ed asked, "You mean you hid your mother out here in the open, all by herself, without a bed or any kind of shelter?"

"Our people do not need beds or roofs," Pablo replied. A touch of scornful pride was in his voice.

"Why didn't you bring her to the house?" Ed asked. "All you needed to do was to tell us you wanted her to come stay with you. We'd've made her welcome."

Pablo said nothing for a moment. When he spoke, it was with a tone of dignified apology. "I was afraid you would not let me do this thing. It is not just for a visit that my mother has come. She has been working in the town, but she grew lonely—none of our people live there now. She wanted to live with me, here."

"I don't see anything wrong with that," Ed said. "A man's got a duty to look after his mother. I guess that's the same whether he's white or Indian. What's her name?"

"My mother is called Maria. You will let her stay, then? She can sleep in the shed with me if you will let her. And she will eat only a little food, I will pay for it."

"We won't worry about that," Ed assured him. "Matter of fact, I sorta imagine Amanda'd like to have another woman on the place. Sure, she can stay, Pablo."

"I am grateful."

"No need to be. You've earned the right. Now, then. Looks like the best thing to do is to get her back to your place and fix up a place for her to sleep. Tomorrow maybe she'd like to come down to the house and get acquainted with Amanda and Nellie. And when there's something you want next time, Pablo, you come talk to me about it. You understand?"

"Yes. And I will not forget."

Chapter
17

A searing, late summer sun beat down on the Bronson claim. It sent bright, stinging shafts of concentrated heat through the thin-branched cottonwood saplings that Ed, in response to Amanda's urging, had transplanted from the riverbottom while the roots were dormant during midwinter. All but a few of the saplings had rooted, their growth stimulated by the plentiful water that seeped from the cistern's overflow pipe and from the mine's sluice box and was channeled by irrigation trenches through the grove. The trees were still small, though, their foliage sparse, and there were more areas of sunlight below them than there were of shade.

Nellie sat on the ground among the trees; she was now learning to sew and with scraps from Amanda's ragbag was fashioning a new dress for Rosie. Until a half hour earlier she'd been in the house finishing up her chores, but once they'd been completed she hurried outside. As hot as it was under the cottonwoods, it was even hotter indoors where the walls cut off the vague whispers of breeze that infrequently passed over the sun-drenched land. Rosie lay on a cushion at Nellie's side where the girl could drape the partly finished dress on the doll and check it for size and fit as the work progressed.

Behind her the house stood silent, its doors and windows open wide, as though the dwelling itself were
gasping for a breath of cool air. Amanda had decided
to go with Ed on his monthly trip to Vadito, but Nellie
had chosen to stay behind and avoid the baking heat of
the dirt road. In the area beyond the cottonwood grove
Pablo and Maria were working the plot of land that Ed
had given them permission to clear for a garden. Pablo
had explained somewhat hesitantly when spring came
that his mother would like to grow some of the foods
to which she was accustomed, maize and squash and
beans. He would help Maria look after the garden,
he'd told Ed, but promised that this would never inter-
fere with his work at the mine or any of the other jobs
Ed gave him to do.

Until she began working the garden plot, getting the
baked earth ready for planting, Maria had been seen
only infrequently by any of the Bronson family. Soon
after she'd moved into the shed with Pablo, Amanda
had asked him if his mother would like to earn a bit of
money by helping with the washing and cleaning. Pablo
had returned with the message that Maria had worked
hard for many years and was very tired; she would not
work for pay, but if Amanda needed her help, she offered it out of gratitude. By Amanda's standards of the
master-servant relationship this was an unacceptable
offer. She did not ask again.

After Ed had approved Maria's request for a garden,
Maria became more visible. She was seen daily, breaking the soil beyond the cottonwood grove, scratching
small trenches to carry part of the overflow water that
pooled in the grove to the bean and squash hills and to
the few rows of maize she planted. Ed had gone to her
once, suggesting that since they were not short of
water, Pablo could dig regular ditches for the garden.

Maria had listened impassively, nodded as though she'd understood his offer, then returned to her work.

"She's a strange one," Ed had commented to Amanda. "Stood there and listened to me without blinking an eye and then just turned aside and went on hoeing like I'd never said a word to her."

"I think she must've had a very hard life," Amanda suggested. "All those scars on her face. Perhaps smallpox or some kind of sickness when she was young."

"Well, if having her here keeps Pablo happy and on the job, I sure don't mind her being around. The little bit she eats don't hurt us a bit, and I'd hate to lose Pablo. That Indian's a real good worker, and he's learned the way I like to see things done. I'd be hard put to find somebody to take his place if he was to leave."

Nellie laid aside the doll dress to watch the Indians working in the harsh sunlight that flooded the garden plot. Her sewing lessons with Amanda had made her suddenly aware of clothing, and she realized with surprise that she'd never seen Pablo wearing anything except the garments he now had on: a denim shirt with tattered cuffs at the end of long sleeves and faded, brown denim jeans. Maria, too, seemed to own no other garments than those she'd been wearing when she first came to live at the claim. She wore an ankle-length calico dress with a petticoat under it, and over the dress, a short, sleeveless jacket.

Nellie herself had on a sleeveless dress of lightweight dimity, one of several that made up her summer wardrobe. She decided she must ask her mother why it was that Indians, who wore the same clothing the year around, were apparently unaffected by the differences between summer and winter temperatures, while whites, who changed from lightweight clothes in summer to heavier garments in winter, were never really

comfortable at either season. There must be some reason, she concluded, some difference between the races
that made it possible for the Indians to work easily in
temperatures that drained the energy from whites.

While these thoughts had been going through her
mind, without really being conscious of it, Nellie had
been watching Maria and Pablo at work. Now she noticed that Pablo had seen her face turned toward them
and was waving to her. She returned the wave. Pablo
put his hoe down, said something to his mother, and
walked toward the cottonwood grove. Several weeks
had passed since he and Nellie had really spoken with
one another, aside from the briefest greetings when Pablo came to the house to get food. Nellie smiled in anticipation of a chat with him; she'd been wondering
whether his mother was happy living on the claim and
whether Pablo felt better for having her with him.

Pablo did not come directly to where Nellie sat, but
walked through the grove and stopped a few yards
away at the cistern. He pushed its wooden cover aside
and drank from his cupped hand. Then he walked up
to Nellie, stopped, and squatted on his heels.

"My mother is pleased that she has a garden," he
volunteered. "It is a long time since she could grow the
things she likes best to eat."

"That's good. And you're happy because she is?"

"This thing is true." Pablo saw the doll and pointed
to it. "Have you been talking to the Rosie again?"

"Oh, I always talk to her. Right now I'm making her
a new dress." Nellie picked up the partly finished doll
garment and held it up. "See how pretty it's going to
look on her?" As she spoke, she reached for the doll,
but her arm was not quite long enough. Instead of
grasping it, her fingers dislodged it from the cushion
and it slipped off to the ground.

Nellie did not hear the almost inaudible tick-tick-tick
that was the warning rattle of the sidewinder. To escape the uncomfortably hot, sun-bathed ground sur-
rounding the trees, the little horned reptile—less than a
foot long, but with venom as potent as its big diamond-
back cousins—had moved earlier in its distinctive sidewise glide into the dappled shade beneath the
cottonwoods. It is the habit of these small desert rattlesnakes to find the cool shelter they must have by
pushing themselves under a thin layer of soil at the
shaded side of a standing rock. This one had inserted
itself in the earth beside the edge of the pillow on
which Rosie lay. The doll falling disturbed the snake,
then its heat sensors were alerted when Nellie's bare
arm passed its head as she reached for the doll. The
sensors triggered the rattler's instinct to strike.

Pablo's desert-sharpened ears heard the sidewinder's
tick-tick start. He knew the reptile's habits and located
it before it had finished its warning rattle. He moved
instantly. His hand shot out and pushed Nellie's arm
away. The sidewinder, rearing up from its concealed
resting place, sank its needle-sharp fangs into Pablo's
forearm.

Two or three seconds are required for a striking rattlesnake to sink its fangs deeply enough into flesh and
press a full load of venom down from poison sacs
above the fangs. Perhaps another second passes before
the fangs retract into their sheaths and free the reptile
from its victim. In those seconds Pablo moved with a
speed that Nellie had never dreamed was possible for
human muscles. She did not really see Pablo's free arm
come up, or his hand grasp the snake and slide down
the sidewinder's slick scales to its tail. All she got was
the impression of motion as the snake fell free and Pablo flicked its head against the ground with a sharp

snap. The rattler went limp as its vertebrae fractured. It was dead, but after Pablo let its body fall to the ground, the sidewinder still twitched in convulsive spasms for several moments.

Maria must have been watching them from the garden plot, Nellie realized later. Almost by the time Pablo had dropped the dead rattlesnake, his mother was at his side. She looked at the sidewinder's still twitching body.

"*Ah-vae hukthar*," she said. Her voice was void of emotion. As she spoke, she extended her open hand to Pablo.

Pablo understood the gesture at once. He passed her the sheath knife which he wore at his belt. Maria slit his shirt-sleeve from wrist to shoulder and as the sleeve dangled free, tore off a strip of the closely woven cloth and quickly twisted it into a makeshift cord. She tied the cord tightly around Pablo's arm just above the elbow, drawing it up so tightly that the cord cut into his flesh. With the tip of the knife Maria slashed deeply across the twin punctures that showed as small dots of blood on her son's forearm and began sucking at the wound.

All these things happened in such quick, bewildering sequence that Nellie saw them without actually being aware of what she was seeing. From the moment that Maria cut Pablo's shirt-sleeve away, Nellie had only been able to stare in stunned, transfixed fascination at the long jagged scar, the shape of a forked lightning-bolt, that had been revealed when Pablo's arm was bared. Nellie had heard the story of Gato too many times not to understand the significance of that scar.

Her startled gasp and the look of fear-filled surprise that transformed her face signaled Nellie's recognition to Pablo. When at last her eyes moved from his scarred forearm to his face, Pablo shook his head slowly.

"But, you—" Nellie began.

Pablo cut her short. "Say nothing. There is a time to speak, but this is not such a time."

Nellie did not try to say more. The full recognition of what she'd discovered was sinking very slowly into her mind because she was willing herself not to believe it.

Maria kept extracting the venom from the opened, fang wound, sucking vigorously and spitting out the mixture of blood and poison. Belief came to Nellie so slowly that when Maria put her arm around her son's waist and began leading him along the path to their shack, Nellie followed them instinctively. The Indian woman turned and said something in her own tongue. Nellie did not understand the words, but the tone of Maria's voice made her meaning clear; its impatient anger told her that Maria wanted no help.

Beads of sweat, the first effects of the venom beginning to course through his blood, began popping out on Pablo's face. He said softly to Nellie, "Do not be afraid. I will not hurt you. Let me go now with my mother. She knows how to treat the bite, she will look after me."

Nellie stopped following the Indians then. She watched their backs as they went slowly up the gentle slope that led to the abrupt towering face of the cliff and were lost to her sight behind the bulking wheel of the *arrastre*. For a long while Nellie stood unmoving, ignoring the heat, staring across the strip of sunlit landscape where no one moved. After a while she went into the house and sat down.

At some point during the hours that passed while she waited for Ed and Amanda to return, Nellie won the struggle to convince herself of the truth, to believe the evidence of what her eyes had seen. Even before twilight deepened and she heard the wagon rattling over the rutted road to the house, Nellie had decided what she must do. She could not bring herself to speed the arrival of that unhappy moment by going to meet her parents, though.

"My lands, Nellie!" Amanda exclaimed. "Sitting here in the dark! You knew we'd be watching for our windows and get worried if we didn't see them lit up. Why didn't you light a lamp?"

There was a sound of scraping as Ed pulled a Walker match through its folded striking paper. The match sparked and smoked while he lifted the chimney of a tablelamp and lighted its wick. The moment the lamp glowed full and her parents could see Nellie's face, they knew something was wrong.

"Looks like you had a reason to worry, Manda," Ed said. "Something bad's happened." Turning to face Nellie, he asked, "What is it, honey? What's got you so upset?"

Nellie felt strangely calm. She did not burst into tears, nor did she blurt out her discovery in one quick, breathless gushing of words. Speaking very slowly, she began a detailed recounting of the afternoon's events. She started from the moment she'd gotten warm indoors and had taken Rosie out to the cottonwood grove. Her story was broken by long pauses during which she tried to bring back from her memory each small incident, but Ed and Amanda sensed that they must not interrupt the girl or try to hurry her.

At the very end after she had told her parents what she saw when Maria slit Pablo's shirt-sleeve and revealed his scarred forearm, but before they could begin to question her, she said plaintively, "I don't see how anybody as nice and quiet as Pablo could be Gato, Papa. But I guess he is, all right. That's exactly the kind of scar the marshal told us to watch for."

"My God!" Ed breathed. "Pablo? Why, he's been as good and hardworking an Indian as I've ever seen. I guess I don't understand how he could be Gato, either."

Amanda had less difficulty in accepting Pablo's double identity. She said, "Now, Ed, Nellie's told you what she saw, and I don't suppose either one of us believes she'd make up a story like that. I'm not real surprised, though. I've had a feeling there was something wrong ever since he tried to sneak his mother in here without telling us about her."

"You're real sure you saw the scar, now?" Ed asked Nellie. She nodded without hesitation, her lips set in a thin, firm line. He said, "Well, I've got to go right back to town, then, and bring Swan. Manda, you and Nellie better come with me. I don't want to risk leaving you out here by yourselves."

"No, Ed. Nellie's not in any condition to make that trip into Vadito. To tell you the truth, I don't feel much like jouncing there and back again, either."

"Now, Manda, be sensible! What about—"

"Gato?" Amanda broke in. "You know what the marshal told us—Gato never harms women." She smiled without mirth. "I'm really serious, Ed. I'm not afraid. Just get the shotgun out of the wagon and leave it here with us."

"Suppose he came down here and tried to break into the house?"

"Then I'd shoot," Amanda replied promptly. "I'll bolt the doors and draw the curtains and if I hear anything moving around outside, I'll shoot, that's all. Besides, you'll get to town a lot quicker riding

Jehoshaphat than you will in a loaded wagon pulled by
two tired mules."

Ed said slowly, "Yes. That makes sense. But before
I saddle up, I'll just go up there and see how the land
lays. If Pablo got a pretty good dose of rattlesnake poison, he's going to be too sick to hurt anybody or even
to move for quite a while. Unless he's already lit out
and has gone into a hidey-hole someplace."

Amanda and Nellie stood at the window and
watched the bobbing glow of the lantern Ed carried.
They followed his progress up the slope, held their
breath when the light disappeared briefly behind the
arrastre, and breathed again when it reappeared and
moved up to the shed. It blinked out momentarily
again, then reappeared and began moving back toward
the house.

"He's there, all right," Ed reported when he came
in. "Clear out of his head with the poison, tossing
around, sweating and mumbling. Maria's sitting by
him. She didn't say anything when I looked in, but I
swear I've never seen such an ugly look on a woman's
face before. I'm not sure but what I'm worse afraid of
her than I am of Pablo."

"If he's all that sick, Maria will be too busy taking
care of him to think about us," Amanda pointed out.
"But from what Nellie told us, he didn't have time to
absorb very much of the venom. That means you'll
have to hurry and get the marshal out here."

"All right," Ed said. "I still don't like the idea of
leaving you, but I guess it's the best way. But you be
careful, you hear?"

Afterward Nellie could never recall anything of the
vigil she and Amanda shared that night except that the
hours seemed to stretch into an endless eternity of
waiting. What they said to one another, or if they said

anything at all, she did not remember. As the night dragged on, she was sure she dozed two or three times, always waking to see her mother sitting motionless and alert in a straight-backed chair, the shotgun resting across her lap.

Dawn was less than an hour away when Ed Bronson got back, accompanied by Hank Swan and four Vadito men the marshal had deputized. Nellie heard the hoofbeats on the rocky wagonroad that had been worn to the house. The mounts pulled up outside and she heard her father say, "Give me a minute to make sure Amanda and Nellie are all right, and I'll show you the path up to the shed."

Amanda stood up as Ed came through the door. She said, "I told you nothing was going to happen to us. Go on with the marshal now and help him get that murdering savage off our place."

"You're sure he's still up at the shed?"

"Not sure, no, but I haven't heard any noises from there. They might've sneaked away, but they can't have gotten very far if they did."

"We'll soon find out."

"Here." Amanda handed Ed the shotgun. "It'll be better than your pistol in the dark."

This time there was no lantern by which Nellie and her mother, watching from the house, could keep track of the progress the men made as they moved quietly up the slope to the shed. They waited for what seemed a very long time before the men's voices reached them through the dark distance in brief spates of unintelligible sounds. A light flared briefly, was visible for the length of time it took for a Walker match to burn itself out, then darkness returned. A woman's voice rose for a moment in loud, angry wailing. Then there was silence.

Stumbling footsteps told them the men were returning. Amanda called into the darkness, "Ed? Are you all right?"

"We're fine, Manda. And it's all over and done with."

Now the group was close enough for Nellie and Amanda to see the men by the dim light leaking through the windows of the house. Ed was leading, and Hank Swan was close behind him. Back of them the others came, bending over, carrying Pablo between them. The Indian's body sagged limply, hanging from their hands.

"Is he hurt?" Nellie heard herself asking.

It was Swan, not her father, who replied. "Nobody's hurt. The Indian's all right, just sick from the snakebite."

Amanda asked, "But where's Maria?"

"We don't want her for anything," Swan answered. "No murders charged against her that I know of."

Ed told Amanda, "I promised the marshal that I'd take her into town in a day or two. Don't worry, Manda. I'll keep a close watch on her, she won't do any harm."

"What will you do with him?" Nellie asked. She couldn't bring herself to say either "Pablo" or "Gato," but knew everybody would understand who she meant.

Swan's voice was soft but emphatic. "Well, soon as we help your pa unload his wagon, we'll haul Gato into Vadito and put him in that new jail the town council just got through building. Then as soon as the governor sends us a judge, he'll go on trial. I sorta imagine the jury's going to find him guilty of murder, and as soon as they do, I reckon we'll hang him. And that'll be the end of it."

Chapter
18

Breakfast that day at the house on the claim had an unreal atmosphere. It was midafternoon before the family sat down to eat, and all three of them had the disquieting feeling that on the previous day Death had brushed past them so closely that the smell of graveyard mould still stuck in their nostrils.

Their edginess showed up in different ways. Amanda burned two batches of pancakes and had to mix fresh batter. Ed cut himself when he shaved. Nellie dropped the full coffeepot on the kitchen floor. The meal was a silent one, the food tasted like straw. It was not until they were almost through eating that Nellie brought up the name all of them had been trying not to think about.

"Papa. Is Mr. Swan really going to hang Pablo like he said last night?"

"I don't imagine the marshal will actually do the hanging. But I don't see how Pablo can get off."

"Can they prove he's really Gato, Ed?" Amanda asked. "Marshal Swan's always said nobody's ever seen Gato and lived long enough to describe him except the one man who told about his scar. And that was a long time ago, when we first came here, remember."

"They'll find some way to prove it, I guess," Ed replied. "Swan was talking on the way out here last night about there being some soldiers at the fort who can swear he's the one who killed some men there. I'd say that's about all they need."

"What's going to happen to Maria?" Nellie frowned. "Last night the marshal said they haven't got anything against her, so does that mean she'll go free?"

"Hard to tell, honey. Anyhow, it's not a thing for you to be vexing yourself with. Best thing to do is forget all about it."

"That's right," Amanda agreed. "Just put it out of your mind. Think about something pleasant. You've got a birthday coming along next month, and a girl deserves a party when she's fifteen. Why don't you think about what's ahead instead of what's past?"

Ed picked up the cue quickly. "Do what your mother says, Nellie. Maybe for your birthday we can all go to Prescott for a few days, see what we can find there for a birthday present. How'd you like that?"

"All right, I guess." But Nellie was not to be distracted. She asked Ed, "Is Maria going to keep on living here?"

"For a little while."

"Oh, no, Ed!" Amanda exclaimed. "I thought the marshal would be taking her into town in a few days."

"Now, stop fretting, Manda. Swan says it's going to take him a while to get things sorted out. He might want to hold her and he might not, but he figures if she's here, a place she's used to, she won't be so likely to run off."

"I hoped we'd be able to start forgetting about all this," Amanda said soberly.

"We will. The woman won't bother you. I'll be working the mine, so I can keep an eye on her, take victuals up to her. It won't be for very long. I sorta figure we owe Pablo that much. Don't forget, if it hadn't been for him sticking out his arm and taking that snakebite for her, Nellie might be dead right now."

"Well." Mollified by Ed's reminder of the sidewinder, Amanda accepted the situation. "I guess it won't hurt anything if she's here another few days."

Through the long, dragging hours of the afternoon Pablo—none of the Bronson family could readily think of him as Gato—remained a ghostly presence in the house. His name was not spoken again, but that he was in their minds was betrayed by the preoccupation all three showed, the desultory manner in which they attended to their different tasks. That night long after the house grew quiet, Nellie could hear the low murmur of voices from her parents' room. With unabashed curiosity she crept silently out of bed and tiptoed to listen at the open door.

Ed was saying, "What Swan's really worried about is that some of the soldiers at Fort Mohave will get all worked up and decide to bust open the jail and take Pablo out and string him up without any kind of trial. Swan says unless the whole Gato story comes out in open court, all the yarns and rumors about him won't ever die down."

"Wouldn't the soldiers get into trouble if they did that? Surely the officers wouldn't close their eyes to them lynching someone."

"They'd be in trouble, but it wouldn't help Pablo, he'd be dead. And if his mother was in jail, too, Swan's afraid they might lynch 'em both."

"What's the marshal doing then?" Amanda asked.

"Well, he sent a man to Prescott to ask the governor to get a judge to Vadito right away so they can have a quick trial. And he's sent a message to the fort to warn the commander to keep his men on a tight rein until things cool down. So that's why I felt like I had to go along with Swan about Maria."

"You could've told me all this before," Amanda said.

"Now, Manda, I was too tired to talk when I got home, and you were too upset to listen. I didn't want to say anything at the table because I was afraid of getting Nellie roiled up more than she already is."

"Yes, I can see it's bothering her pretty badly."

"I don't feel so good about it myself, Manda. Mainly I guess I'm mad because I let Pablo pull the wool over my eyes for such a long time."

"I wasn't exactly thinking of that. Nellie's at a funny stage in growing up, Ed. Part baby girl, part woman. I remember a little bit about how I was at her age, and it worries me."

"What're you getting at, Manda?"

"Oh, I used to imagine outlandish things about half the boys in town, even boys I'd never talked to except to say hello. I'd dream about me being in some kind of trouble and them rescuing me, like the prince in a fairy story."

"I can't see Nellie imagining an Indian hired man being a fairy prince."

"Can't you? Remember, Nellie hasn't had any playmate except her doll. And think back, how she sat up there day after day watching you and Pablo at work on the *arrastre*, and the same thing when you were building the house. Then when that snake yesterday—"

"Now, you're just imagining things, Manda. Why, Nellie and Pablo never said more than three words to one another."

"I suppose I am borrowing trouble. But I worry."

"Sure you do. Sometimes you worry too much."

"Ed. Do you think we ought to build a house in

Vadito later on and live there part of the time? Or send Nellie off to school, someplace where she'd have a chance to be around other people?"

"Maybe." Ed yawned audibly. "We'll talk about it later on after this mess settles down."

Her parents' bedroom grew quiet and after a moment or two Nellie crept back to her own bed. Ed's mention of lynching had alarmed her; she recalled lynchings being discussed in hushed whispers as dreadful punishments. Nellie could not visualize Pablo as the merciless, wanton killer known as Gato. Her image of Gato was a huge Indian with red glaring eyes in a hate-contorted face who crept up behind his victims and laughed while blood poured from their throats after he'd slashed them. Pablo she knew. He was a brown, friendly face working beside her father, a hand reaching out with interested curiosity to touch Rosie's hair, a pair of black eyes looking at her with serious wonder as she chattered away during the few times they'd talked together. Pablo was an arm imposed between her and a striking rattlesnake.

There'd been a mistake, Nellie tried to convince herself. Somewhere roaming the desert was the real Gato, a fearsome Indian with a scar like the one Pablo had. The consolation failed. Nellie could not hide from herself the sober truth that Pablo was indeed Gato, and the truth was more painful because she had been the one to reveal it. Worse, the revelation had been made while Pablo was suffering the effects of a bite of the snake from which he'd saved her. Nellie felt very alone. She could not ask her parents to help her save Pablo from lynching nor could she think of anyone else to whom she could turn. She was still trying to think of a way by which she could help him when sleep overcame her.

It was Ed who unintentionally gave Nellie the idea
that had eluded her night thoughts when at breakfast
he reminded Amanda that he'd need food to carry to
Maria when he went up to the mines. Later in the
morning, her household chores done, Nellie picked up
Rosie and started up the path. Her mother saw her go,
but Nellie's departure with the doll was an almost daily
occurrence, something too commonplace to be noted.

She was not doing anything wrong, Nellie repeated
to herself as she walked toward the *arrastre*, she was
not really sneaking off behind her parents' backs.
They'd be angry if they knew, of this Nellie was aware,
but her urge to talk to Maria was greater than her
concern about facing their scolding. She looked around
for Ed, but he was in the mine tunnel. Nellie hurried to
the toolshed and slipped inside, closing the door behind
her.

.Maria sat on the floor in the angle formed by the
two bunkbeds that had been built foot-to-foot in one
corner of the shed and were its only furnishings. A
plate of food, untouched, lay on the floor near the Indian woman. She looked up when Nellie entered, but
did not speak. .

"Maria," Nellie said, "I want to help you and Pablo."

Maria did not answer, but looked fixedly at the girl.
Nellie. waiting for a reply, stared back. She was surprised that Maria looked so young; she had always
given Nellie the impression of age. Even in the dim
light of the windowless shed Nellie could see that
Maria's face bore few wrinkles, but she was deeply
scarred around mouth and chin. Her arms and hands,
too, were marked by deep pits of long-healed wounds.
Nellie wondered if Maria had understood, if she even
spoke English.

"I want to help," the girl repeated. "Me. Help. You and Pablo." She gazed at Maria, her hopeful expression changing to one of despair when no reply followed her offer. Maria's expression had not changed. Nellie said, "Oh, dear! I guess you just don't understand what I'm saying, do you?"

"I understand," Maria replied. "Why?"

"Why what?"

"Why help. You *hyko* woman, help your people. Not us."

"No, no!" Nellie protested. "Pablo saved me from the rattlesnake. If he hadn't been helping me, nobody would have found out about him. Don't you see, I've got to help him if I can."

"No can. All chase him, long time. Now they catch him, kill him."

"That's what I'm trying to say. They can't kill him unless they can prove Pablo's really Gato and that he killed those people."

"How prove?"

"Somebody will have to swear, tell the judge, that they saw Pablo kill somebody. Or saw him close to where there was a killing. And maybe if you knew he didn't, you could tell the judge—"

"They say I lie, he my son."

Nellie realized that Maria was probably right. She grasped at the straw she had left. "Maria, if your son did kill somebody, and they'd hurt him first or done him some wrong, the judge might be easier on him. But you'd have to tell them how everything started."

"Who think I speak true?"

"I would. And if I believe you, the judge might, too." Then without really intending to, Nellie asked the question that had been haunting her mind. "Tell me the truth, Maria. Is Pablo really Gato?"

"No. Not Gato." Nellie's eyes brightened, but their glow faded when Maria went on. "Not Pablo. He, Hahksle. Me, not Maria. Kahenee. Cocopah."

"That's his real name, his Indian name?" Nellie struggled with the pronunciation. "Hahksle?" Maria nodded. "And yours is Kahenee?" Another nod. Nellie persisted in her probing for the answer she hadn't received. "But did he really kill a lot of men?"

Kahenee smiled, a singular smile that somehow managed to convey sly secretiveness, pleasure, triumph, and sadness. Her voice was low as she said, "Hahksle a man. He do what man must do to be man."

"But why, Maria? Why did he kill somebody?"

"Why? Too long ago, why."

"Maybe—" Nellie thought aloud, "maybe if you could tell me why, I could tell the judge. He'd believe me."

Kahenee's obsidian eyes sought Nellie's green ones. She asked, "This thing you say is true thing?"

"That I'd tell the judge? And that if the judge knew why Pablo had killed somebody, it might help him? Of course it's true. But—maybe I'd tell Marshal Swan first and have him tell the soldiers. Papa says they might break in and"—she hesitated—"and hurt Pablo before the judge gets here."

"Soldiers!" Maria spat. "Hahksle hate soldiers!"

"But tell me why he does, Maria."

Nellie's young sincerity and her persistence brought Kahenee to a decision. "I tell." She patted the bunk bed beside her. "Sit. You be here long time."

Kahenee's story was long in the telling, made longer by her need to pause frequently and search for the words of the unfamiliar language that would translate for Nellie the experience buried in memory. It was a story that Nellie would not forget. Beginning with the

day when she went out from the Cocopah village to
pick pitahaya apples, Kahenee took Nellie back to a
time and a way of life that the young white girl had
never known existed.

It was also a story destined to remain forever unfin-
ished. Absorbed in Kahenee's narration, Nellie forgot
to keep track of the passing time, and at the point
when Kahenee was telling how Hahksle had taken his
revenge for the ruined garden, the door of the toolshed
was opened abruptly and her father's voice brought
Nellie back from the past.

"So here's where you are!" Ed snapped. "Me and
your mother was just about to ride into town and have
the marshal organize a posse to come help us look for
you! What're you doing up here with this woman, Nellie?"

"Papa, I'm sorry I forgot to notice how long I've
been away from the house. I was just trying to find out
what made"—Nellie hesitated imperceptibly—"what
made Pablo do the things he did."

Ed ignored Nellie's explanation. "Your mother's half
out of her mind from worry! You'd be better off spend-
ing your time trying to help her than sneaking off to
listen to a woman that spawned a skulking killer!"

"But, Papa—"

"Don't 'but Papa' me! Get yourself down to the
house! Your ma'll have something to say to you!"

Nellie's last memory of Kahenee was a pair of jet
eyes in a scarred, young-old face, caught in a fleeting
glimpse as Ed led her from the toolshed.

Amanda's scolding was more temperate than Ed's
had been. Amanda spoke softly but with feeling of the
dangers that come with careless associations and of
foolish thoughts that come to young inexperienced girls
who have not yet learned to form adult judgment. The

lecture was capped by a sentence of bed immediately without supper and confinement to the house for a week.

Nellie's disappointment that she would not hear the rest of Kahenee's story vanished the next morning together with her hope of helping Pablo. Ed burst into the kitchen, the plate of food he'd taken to the toolshed still in his hand. Angrily he said, "The woman's gone! Must've picked up and skipped out during the night!"

"Good riddance of bad rubbish!" Amanda replied feelingly. "I never would've rested easy as long as she stayed on the place."

Ed was still angry. "Good riddance for you maybe. Not so good for me. I'll lose a day's production riding to tell the marshal she's got away, and I'll feel like a fool after telling him I promised to keep an eye on her."

Hank Swan had not seemed too put out by Kahenee's disappearance; however, Nellie overheard Ed telling Amanda after he'd gotten back from Vadito later in the day.

"Swan just nodded when I told him," Ed said. "Sorta like he'd looked for her to sneak off the way she did. Said it wasn't nothing for me to worry over, that he wasn't planning on putting any charge against her, anyhow."

Amanda sighed. "Well. I guess we've seen the last of both of them. And I'm glad. Now maybe things will settle back to normal around here, and we can all sleep peacefully at night."

Life on the claim did settle down, but the period of calm was short. Three days after Kahenee disappeared, as Amanda and Nellie were washing the last of the breakfast dishes, thudding hooves on the trail to the house sent them out on the porch to see who was arriving in such haste. Neither of them recognized the rider who pulled his horse to a hoof-thumping halt and leaped from the saddle.

"This the Bronson claim?" the man demanded. When Amanda nodded, he went on. "Then you'd be Miz Bronson. I got a message from Marshal Swan for your husband. Marshal wants him to saddle up and get to town quick as he can. Gato's got away!"

Chapter
19

"Got away!" Ed exclaimed after he'd run down from the mine in response to Amanda's ringing the "come home" signal with the dinner bell. "How in hell could he get out of a locked cell with iron bars across the window and door?"

Swan's messenger explained, "Well, Hank guessed the night deputy dozed off long enough for somebody to sneak in off the street and take the key down from where it was hanging on the wall and unlock the cell door."

"What do you mean, Swan 'guesses' that's what happened? What did the night deputy say?"

"He couldn't talk. The day man found him this morning laying on the floor with his head all bashed in and his shotgun gone."

"Dead?"

"No. But he's pretty close to being from what I heard."

Amanda said, "It was Maria. She must've opened the cell door."

"Probably was her, all right," Ed agreed. "Couldn't've been anybody else wanting to get him out of jail. She must've hiked into town when she left here, spent a day or so spying on the jail, and then done it last night." He turned to the messenger. "Why'd Swan send for me? There's plenty of people in Vadito he can call on for help getting up a posse. If I go in, I'd have to leave my wife and little girl out here alone or take 'em in with me."

"Hank says you know the country better'n most of them folks in town. And you're one who'll recognize Gato if you see him. He said tell you he's counting on you to help."

"When's the posse riding out?" Ed asked.

"Soon as the Pima tracker Hank's sent for gets there from the fort."

Bronson shook his head. "No. While I'm chasing over half the territory, suppose Gato would head back here and find my womenfolk alone? You go back and tell Swan I'm going to look after what's mine."

"Wait a minute, Ed," Amanda broke in. "This is the last place in the world Pablo would come back to because he's smart enough to know it's the first place anybody'd look for him. I think you ought to go on and help the marshal."

"I won't do it, Manda. It's too risky for you and Nellie."

"Pooh!" she snorted. "Just leave the shotgun with me. It'd be risky for Pablo to come back, not for us."

"But this might be a three- or four-day job," Ed protested. "Or even longer if Pablo's got much of a start."

"That's why you ought to go," Amanda said firmly. "If that Indian isn't caught right now, he might run loose for another two or three years. Nobody's going to feel safe as long as he's free. Now, you go ahead. Nellie and I will be all right."

"Well—" Ed was wavering. "If you're sure."

"I'm sure."

"All right, then." He nodded to Swan's messenger.

"I'll be with you as soon as I get my guns and saddle up."

If Amanda felt any fear during the long vigil that began with Ed's departure for Vadito, Nellie saw no sign of it. As far as possible her mother kept the girl busy with the usual household routine and when regular chores were done, invented a few new jobs to occupy their time. The only disturbance to their normal pattern was the frequency with which Amanda interrupted her work to go to the door and to make the rounds of the windows, scanning the countryside. Always, of course, both Nellie and her mother were aware of the buckshot-loaded, double-barreled shotgun that lay across the kitchen table, its hammers at full cock.

After the two had eaten supper in silence, Amanda said, "We'll set out lanterns at the corners of the house before it gets dark. Get the coal oil can while I lift the lanterns down off the shelf. We've got to fill them to make sure they'll burn all night. If that Indian comes prowling around, I want to see him before he gets too close."

Nellie had expected to join her mother for the night watch, but as soon as the lanterns had been set out and the sky darkened down into twilight, Amanda said, "All right, young lady, it's off to bed for you. Now, sleep sound and don't worry. I'll be keeping watch."

"But, Mama—"

"No fussing, now, and no back talk. I told you to go to bed."

Nellie had heard that tone in Amanda's voice before; it meant that there was to be no argument, and reluctantly she obeyed. Twice during the night she awakened as she heard her mother moving from one window to another, peering out, trying to penetrate the shadows that seemed to crouch menacingly beyond the light cast by the lanterns. The night passed quietly, though.

Late in the morning Amanda began to show the strain of her all-night watch. Her eyelids sagged, her brisk step slowed. At last she said, "Nellie, I need to rest my eyes a few minutes, but I'm sure we'll be safe. If Pablo was going to come here at all, it'd have been while it was dark. He's probably miles away by now, running from the posse. But you keep a good lookout and call me if you see anything at all."

For a while after Amanda fell asleep, Nellie moved from window to window, following the pattern her mother had set during the night. When time after time her attentive inspections showed nothing, the routine that had been exciting became boring. She went to her room, got Rosie and her sewing basket, and went out on the porch. She sat down and started to work on the doll's dress, untouched since her escape from the sidewinder.

Engrossed in the fine seamwork of the miniature dress, Nellie forgot her surroundings and lost track of time. Reaching for her scissors to clip a thread, she raised her eyes from her work and gasped in astonishment. Less than ten feet away Pablo stood watching her.

Before Nellie could speak, he put a hand across his lips to signal silence. In the other hand he held a shotgun. When he saw that Nellie was not going to cry out or speak, he stepped closer. A yard apart they gazed silently at one another. Pablo still wore the clothes he'd had on when Nellie last saw him, worn jeans, tattered shirt with a sleeve cut away. On his bared arm a scruffy bandage hid most of the identifying scar.

It was Pablo's face that made him look so different,

Nellie decided. She was not looking now at the smooth, calmly impassive features she remembered. His eyes were sunk deeply into their sockets and almost hidden by slitted lids that allowed only a narrow strip of his black pupils to show. Around his eyes the skin was striated by a maze of threadlike lines. Deep grooves ran from each nostril to the corners of his mouth, and his lips showed only as a thin, tight line. The effect was a face that had been hewed from hard brown flintrock by an unskilled sculptor.

His voice so low that Nellie could barely hear it, Pablo whispered, "I will not hurt you. They are close behind me, and I must have a water gourd before I go into the desert."

"Where are you going?" Nellie's voice was as soft as Pablo's.

"Far. I will not see this place again. Will you give me water?"

"Of course."

Nellie rememberd that Ed's water gourds were inside and indicated that she would have to go into the house for them. Pablo nodded and signaled for her to hurry. The gourds were hanging on a nail just inside the door; over the leather thong that connected the two gourds and on the same nail hung one of her father's work jackets. Nellie took down the jacket to get to the carrying-thong and was about to hang the jacket back up when she remembered Pablo's torn and ragged shirt.

She took jacket and gourds outside and handed them to Pablo. He stepped to the cistern and filled the gourds, replaced their stoppers. He shrugged into the jacket and was lifting the gourds to his shoulder when he froze and cocked his head, listening. Nellie strained to listen, too, but several moments went by before she could hear the distant rattle of hooves on stony ground and the faint shouts of excited men. By then Pablo was already moving away.

"They are too close," he told her. He waved, a gesture she took as good-bye, and started running up the path toward the cliff.

Nellie watched Pablo until he vanished behind the *arrastre*. The noise of the posse was growing louder very fast. Pablo had barely gotten out of her sight before the riders appeared, Swan at their head, a Pima tracker running afoot in front of the marshal's buckskin.

Swan pulled up and called to Nellie, "Gato was here, wasn't he?"

Almost before the marshal finished the question, Ed Bronson reined Jehoshaphat out of the group of riders and commanded, "Tell him the truth, now, Nellie."

"Yes," she said to Swan. "He was here."

Amanda appeared, the shotgun under her arm. She was not yet fully awake and was rubbing her eyes, bewildered by the commotion.

"How long ago?" Swan asked.

"Just a few minutes. He asked for water." Nellie faced her father, her lips thinned. For a moment she looked like her mother when Amanda was facing an unpleasant task. She went on, "I was afraid not to give it to him, Papa. And he took your water gourds."

"You did right," Bronson said. "No telling what he'd've done if—"

Swan interrupted them. "Which way'd Gato head out?" Nellie indicated the path. The Pima tracker was already moving along it toward the cliff. Swan shouted, "Let's go, men!"

Amanda called, "Ed!"

Bronson was already riding with the others. They reached the cliff and dismounted; the horses could not

take the narrow path that led up to the shed. Nellie
watched the men scattering out, some going into the
mine, others following the tracker around the face of
the cliff.

Amanda looked at Nellie. She said angrily, "I'd like
to know why you didn't wake me up when you saw
that Indian coming toward the house."

"But I didn't see him, Mama! I just looked up and
there he stood!"

"I'll tend to you later, young lady. It's God's wonder
you didn't get both of us killed!"

Amanda had been trying to scold Nellie and watch
the posse at the same time. She gave up on the scolding as she saw the men coming back down the cliff.
They got to the horses and mounted up. Amanda
sighed with relief when her husband came back down
the trail while the others rode around the base of the
cliff.

Bronson pulled up in front of the porch. "Guess
you've already figured, he got away. But he's not far
off. I'm going on with the others. You keep a close
watch, now, you hear? It's not likely he'll come back
with us right on his heels, but he might double."

He turned the mule, ignoring Amanda when she
called to him, and pushed Jehoshaphat on the trail of
Swan and the posse.

At first where Gato's footsteps led through the loose
soil at the base of the cliff, the Pima tracker had no
difficulty. Just beyond the cliff the trail became harder
to follow. Gato had dropped down into an arroyo that
slashed through the hard earth, and the riders had to
wait while the Pima scrambled down its steep side to
find out which way the tracks led at the bottom. The
tracker eventually reappeared a quarter-mile distant in
the direction of the river, and the men spurred to join

him. Wordlessly the Pima pointed northwest toward the distant gorge through which the Colorado ran.

"Swing wide and scatter out!" Swan commanded. "Maybe we can cut him off before he gets too far ahead of us!"

Strung out in single file, the posse swept down to the mouth of the arroyo and swung into a wide-spaced line, moving in the direction of the gorge. They outdistanced the Pima, and when they'd covered more than two miles from the arroyo mouth with no sign of Gato, Swan stopped them. They bunched and waited for the tracker to catch up, letting the horses breathe after their run. Then they waited still longer while the tracker crossed and recrossed the stretch of almost level ground that lay between the arroyo mouth and the break where the first drop into the river canyon began. He finally found enough of a trace to assure them that Gato was heading for the river.

Swan said when they reached the drop-off, "Charley, you stay with the horses. They can't make it down that wall. Maybe we can't do it afoot, I just don't know. We got to try, though. The rest of you take your guns and gourds and whatever hard food you've got in your saddlebags. Whether the trail leads us upstream or down, Charley can see us from up here and lead the horses along."

Skidding, grabbing for holds to keep from falling down the almost vertical drops they encountered, the posse followed the Pima into the canyon of the Colorado. Swan kept urging them to hurry, reminding them they didn't have to keep under cover for fear Gato might pick them off; all he had was a shotgun, and their rifles gave them the advantage of range.

They pushed as fast as they could down the precipitous slope. The going ranged from difficult to impos-

sible. Time after time what looked like a little wrinkle
cutting across the steep downslope turned out to be an
arroyo too wide to jump across and too steep to
scramble in and out of. Time after time they had to
swing wide around stretches of crumbly limestone that
from a distance looked like solid rock. No matter how
hard they tried to hurry, the going was slow. Ahead of
them the Pima zigzagged, reading in the faint streaks
of disturbed soil the footprints left by their still unseen
quarry.

Halfway down the canyon the men were strung out
singly and in pairs when a rifle cracked ahead of them
and a slug kicked up a dustcloud just in front of Swan.
The posse scattered quickly, the men taking cover behind boulders and rock shelves, but no second shot followed.

"That sure as hell wasn't no shotgun load, Marshal!"
one of them called to Swan.

Another asked, "Where'd he get the rifle? Bronson,
did he pick it up at your place?"

"Couldn't have. I'm carrying the only rifle I got."
Then in afterthought, "He might've had one cached,
though, up around that shed where he stopped. That
might be why he went back, to get it."

From behind the boulder where he crouched, Swan
called, "No matter where he got it, he's got it now.
We'll just have to move more careful, stay under cover
as much as we can. At least we got him located now!"

Twice more before the day was over, they had to
scramble for cover when Gato fired sniping shots. After the second shot Swan ordered the posse to hang
back while he and the Pima circled and tried to get
ahead of Gato. When the posse started moving again
and a third slug whined into the boulders, Swan was
waiting upslope. He got off two quick shots. When the

men moved on after waiting a few minutes, Gato did not fire again.

"I'm pretty sure I winged him with my second shot," Swan told them when they were together again. "He lurched, but he didn't fall or stop, and then I lost him in the rocks."

Led by the Pima to the place where Gato had been, they found a blood-trail, bright crimson drops already drying to black on pink and white stones. The Pima led them along the blood-trail for almost two miles before darkness stopped their pursuit.

There was no question of giving up. They camped for the night, a fireless camp, and shared the scraps of jerky and hard-cured sausage and parched corn that they'd grabbed from their saddlebags. Between them they had enough water for a scant swallow apiece while still holding some in reserve against the following day.

With daylight the Pima picked up the trail. They followed doggedly, for the sign was clear that Gato had kept moving during the night. While darkness had kept them immobilized, he'd increased his lead from a few minutes to eight or nine hours.

Late in the afternoon Swan reluctantly called off the chase. Gato had kept to the side of the Colorado gorge, and since midmorning the Pima had been forced to circle every few hundred feet to pick up the trail on the solid rock and hardpan stretches in which it disappeared. The blood-trail had petered out long since, an hour after they'd resumed pursuit.

Swan indicated the brown river almost three miles below them. Between the water and the spot where they were standing. a maze of shallow, eroded canyons, gigantic boulders, small mesas, and long stretches of vertical drops and bulging cliffs marked the terrain.

"There's not much use pushing on," the marshal said. His voice rasped; for the past two hours they'd shared what water remained in their gourds or canteens. The sparing sips they'd taken were never enough to cut the raw dryness of their throats or to replace the moisture that the pitiless sun drew from their bodies in sweat.

Swan went on, "It'd take us the rest of the day to get down there and get the water we'd need to stay on his trail, and most of tomorrow morning to get back here."

"We going to try later when we can come outfitted?" one of the possemen asked.

"I am. If any of the rest of you want to come along, you're welcome. But I'm going to be back on Gato's trail at sunup tomorrow, and I don't plan to give it up until I find him dead or bring him back alive!"

Chapter
20

When we drove up to the neat, gray- and white-painted house, it was late in the morning. Sheriff Carter pulled the big Studebaker touring car to a stop and waved at the old man who was spading his rosebushes in front of the house.

"That's him," he told us. "Hank Swan. He's got a right to hear your story first."

We got out, Carter leading us to where Swan stood. He'd stopped work and was leaning on his garden fork, waiting for us to get to him. Carter said, "Morning, Sheriff."

Swan grinned. "You got your signals crossed again, Fred. The only sheriff I know of in this country is you."

"Hank, you know I called you 'sheriff' too long when I was a youngster to break the habit now," Carter replied. "I'd like you to meet Brad Powers and Al Martin. They're surveying grade for that new spur the Santa Fe's going to build up the river gorge to connect with the Las Vegas & Tonopah."

Al and I shook hands with Swan. He didn't seem too curious about the reason the sheriff had brought us to see him. He looked us over with clear gray eyes shielded by wrinkled, drooping lids. "I'd say you boys just got out of the Army. You see service overseas?"

"Both of us," Al told him.

I added, "We both got a whiff of gas in that last drive in the St. Mihiel salient, so we were mustered out faster than most of our buddies. And the doctor told us to find outside work someplace where the air's clean."

"You won't find air much cleaner than it is here," Swan said. "Well. Come on in if we're going to visit. I was just getting ready to knock off, the sun's too high for comfort now."

He led the way inside. The house was small and square, as houses are in places where lumber is scarce and costly. A single room spanned its front, and through open doors we could see a bedroom in the back on one side, a kitchen on the other. The big living room was uncluttered. A huge Indian rug covered most of the floor. Bordering it stood a sofa with a big lounge chair across from it, a table beside the chair. Near the door wall pegs supported a rifle, the blue rubbed off most of its barrel. On the next peg a holstered pistol dangled from a gunbelt; and a big, creamy Stetson hung on a third peg.

Carter settled on the sofa, motioning Al and me to sit by him. Swan took the easy chair. The sheriff said, "The reason I brought these fellows to see you is to give you the chance to close a case that was still open when you retired."

Swan frowned thoughtfully. "That can't be, Fred. The only case I never did close goes back to the time I was a federal marshal." He stopped, his jaw dropped. "Gato! You mean these men have finally found Gato?"

"I can't be sure, but I'm guessing they did," Carter answered. "We're on the way now to take a look. Thought you'd like to come, too."

Swan didn't bother to answer. He stood up, walked to the door, and put on his hat. He reached for the gunbelt and had his hand on it before he drew back and turned with a sheepish grin to say, "I guess it's habit. I do it damn near every time I start to go out. Well, Fred, what're we waiting on?"

Carter drove the big touring car out from Kingman on the narrow highway north. Swan sat in the front seat with him; Al and I were in back. Swan's eyes stayed half-closed for the first dozen miles, then he turned to Carter and said, "It scares me a little bit when I think about how long ago it was. I lost Gato in '66. Fifty-four years ago. Two wars and a hell of a lot more between then and now."

"It must've been pretty wild country then," Al suggested. "It's wild enough for me now in 1920, but I can imagine what it was like back in 1866."

"It's tamed a lot, though," Swan said, swivelling to look at us. "But we managed. This part didn't really start growing till '82 when the Santa Fe came in. Hell, we didn't have telephones then and not even a telegraph until the railroad got here. No cars, of course, and no roads for 'em if we'd had any. If I'd had what Fred's got today, it sure wouldn't've taken me till now to close the book on Gato."

I was curious, of course, and I knew Al was, at the reference to something neither of us knew about. I said, "You didn't seem surprised when the sheriff told you why we went to him." Then I realized to my own surprise that Carter hadn't said more than that one word, "Gato." I went on, "Come to think of it, he didn't tell you anything at all."

"He didn't have to," Swan replied. "I knew."

Still, neither he nor Carter offered to explain, and by the time we'd driven another thirty minutes with the hot air drying the sweat off four faces before it formed, I was beginning to get a little angry.

We reached the spot where Al and I had left our Ford earlier in the morning, and Al told Carter where to turn off. The sheriff pulled the car up on the big hogback that rose by the highway, and the porous, pink-and-cream decomposing rock crunched under our wheels as we chugged up to the top of the rise. We got out—and stood for a minute or so, stretching our legs, looking down into the river gorge. The hogback dropped off sharply on its western side to reveal the rims of minor canyons zigzagging through protruding buttes and small abrupt mesas. Beyond the broken country a long stretch of level sandy soil sloped gently down to where the brassy glint of the Colorado River tossed back the sun's rays.

Carter asked, "Is the place hard to get to? I've got rope in the car if we need it."

"Well—" I began.

Swan broke in. "Don't say yes unless you mean it, son. I may be eighty-five, but I can still keep up."

"If we need rope, I'll come back for it," Carter decided.

Swan and the sheriff stood aside to let Al and me lead the way. The going was slow, but not as slow as it had been when we'd first gone down in the early morning. We stayed in single file down the steep slope of the hogback's porous rock that gave us holes we could work a foot into and a hand could reach into and grab. Al and I kept looking back nervously, but Swan kept up, just as he'd said he would, while we worked our way down twenty feet to the ledge. It was just a thin scar cut by wind and water that wavered across the face of the cliff. In places it narrowed so sharply that we had to move with our feet splayed out at right angles.

Abruptly the ledge widened into a fairly wide shelf

on which we could walk almost normally. We stopped at the opening we'd made, and Swan edged up close to us. The wall of stones had been laid head-high and extended eight or ten feet along the face of the cliff. We'd taken down only the topmost layers, so the wall was about breast-high as we stood peering into the cave.

"I spotted the place through my transit," Al explained. "It's got a forty-power lens, you know, showed up the walled-in spot real clear."

"Doesn't look like you went inside," Swan observed.

"No, sir," I told him. "We just pulled out enough of the rocks so we could look in and then we saw—well, the body. The sun was back of the bluff then, and we couldn't tell much about it except that it was a dead man. We thought we'd better get the sheriff out here before we went inside. We've heard so much talk about lost mines and prospector's caches—"

"Sure," Swan nodded. "Well, I can tell you pretty much what's in there. A rifle and a shotgun and a pair of water gourds. Maybe a sack with a little grub in it."

"And Gato," Carter added.

"Yes," the old man nodded. "And Gato."

Al and I got busy and pulled away enough of the rock wall so that we could step inside the cave. We let Swan go in first, then the sheriff, and then Al and I crowded in. It was dark and still, and none of us said anything. We just stood looking at the corpse.

Clawlike hands grasped the rifle, holding its dry, cracked stock slanted across extended legs. The head lolled back against the cave's rocky wall, revealing thin lips drawn away from strong yellow teeth in a wide rictal grin. The nose was pinched to a sharp line between eyelids that had drawn tautly together and sealed the sockets which formed round depressions in the thinly covered skull. The cheekbones jutted high and prominent above jaws on which crinkled skin lay no thicker than tissue paper. A red headband of woven cloth was barely visible under a cascade of coarse black hair that spilled down and spread abundantly over bony shoulders.

An unbuttoned jacket of coarse duck was draped over the body's upper torso, and the legs were sheathed in frayed jeans. The jacket gaped open in front, revealing an expanse of skin, wrinkled and taut at the same time, that stretched across a broad chest in which the breastbone and each rib stood out in clear definition. The ribs looked like crossbows drawn up to fire, they arced so sharply. The feet were bare, toes spread apart, the toenails curved like talons. A pair of moccasins lay close to the feet. They were stiff with the dryness of age and looked brittle.

Swan slid the rifle out of the clawed fingers. He said, "Just what I figured, old .45-.70 Army issue." He levered the breech open. The action was stiff with caked, dried grease, but it worked. The gun ejected an unfired cartridge. He handed the rifle to Carter and picked up the shotgun. He broke it and from its chambers two brass shells tumbled out. One had been fired, the other hadn't. The old man grunted and closed the shotgun's breech.

Leaning on the shotgun, he bent over the body again and pulled the jacket's collar flap away from the torso. Bare bone glowed white in the cave's dimness. The shoulder socket and part of the collarbone showed in an area bare of flesh. Swan pushed a finger through a hole in the jacket.

"Thought so," he said. "I was sure I had him square in my sights when I took the last shot at him."

When Swan pulled his finger out of the bullet hole, the jacket twitched sharply. A gleam of bright gold flashed in the dim light and tumbled to the rock floor beside the body. Swan picked it up.

"I'll be damned," he muttered. "It's Rosie."

"Rosie?" Carter asked. There was surprise in his voice.

"Nellie's doll. Nellie Kelly—she was Nellie Bronson then. You know her, Fred. I remember the first time I saw her, she must've been about ten or eleven years old. She was holding the doll. Rosie. The first thing she ever said to me was, 'I purely love Rosie.' Funny how a thing like that sticks in your mind."

"Why?" Carter asked. "Why'd Gato have Rosie?"

Swan shook his head. "I don't know. There's only one time he could've got it. That day he broke jail he hit out for the Bronson claim. But me and the posse couldn't't've been ten minutes behind him." He shook his head again; we could see his mind turning inward. "But Nellie never said anything about missing it. Might be Gato thought Rosie was Nellie's medicine, figured it might rub off on him, help him get away. Or—well, maybe he just wanted something to remember her by."

"That's not likely, is it?" Carter asked. "She must've still been a little girl then. And white to boot."

"We'll find out," Swan said. "Nellie's still living on the old Bronson claim, and it's on the way back to town. We talked about Gato sometimes, Nellie and me, after all the fuss died away. There were a lot of things we wondered about. Where Gato's mother went. Why he was so quiet for such a long time when he worked for Ed Bronson, then all of a sudden took to killing again. Nellie told me a lot I didn't know. But she never mentioned Rosie."

"It's been a long time," Carter said. "And you finally got your man."

Swan shook his head. "No. Not the way I wanted to. Gato got himself a lot more'n I got him."

Carter broke the long silence that followed. "Well, Hank, Gato's still your case as far as I'm concerned. What do you want me to do?"

Swan didn't answer at once. Then he said slowly, "One thing I'd like is for us to stop and give Rosie back to Nellie when we head for town. If these two young fellows don't mind listening to her and me talk about Gato and how it was fifty years and more ago."

Without hesitating I answered for both of us, "We'd like to hear the whole story, Mr. Swan. If you and the sheriff don't mind us listening while you're talking to the lady the doll belongs to."

"It might be a long story," Swan said. "But I don't mind."

"Nor me," Carter agreed. "It all happened so long ago, I'm not certain I know all of it myself." He indicated the body. "What about him? You want me to send a couple of deputies to bring him to town?"

Swan asked, "You still say it's my case?" When the sheriff nodded, he went on, "Send your men out, but just tell 'em to wall up the cave the way it was. Whether he was all bad or part good, Gato's been laying here more'n fifty years. There's not many men have the privilege of choosing where they want to die and rest through all eternity. Even after my bullet hit him, Gato could still have got away. He didn't choose to, he decided he wanted to die right here. I guess he's earned the right to stay."